Jean Teulé lives in the Marais with his companion, the French film actress Miou-Miou. An illustrator, film maker and television presenter, he is also the prize-winning author of more than ten books including *The Suicide Shop* and *The Hurlyburly's Husband*.

Melanie Florence teaches at The University of Oxford and translates from the French.

The Poisoning Angel

The Poisoning Angel

Jean Teulé

Translated from the French by Melanie Florence

Gallic Books
London

A Gallic Book

First published in France as *Fleur de Tonnerre* by Éditions Julliard, 2013

Copyright © Éditions Julliard, Paris, 2013

English translation copyright © Gallic Books 2014

First published in Great Britain in 2014 by Gallic Books, 59 Ebury Street, London, SW1W 0NZ

A CIP record for this book is available from the British Library

ISBN 978-1-908313-68-3

Typeset in Fournier MT by Gallic Books

Printed in the UK by CPI Group (UK) Ltd, Croydon, CR0 4YY

2 4 6 8 10 9 7 5 3 1

Every region has its madness. Brittany has all of them.
Jacques Cambry, founder of the Académie celtique in 1805

Plouhinec

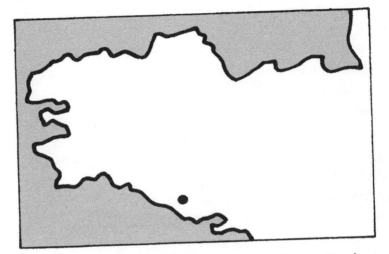

'Oh, no, don't pick that, Hélène, it's a thunderflower. Goodness, that's what I should call you from now on: "Thunderflower". And don't pull on that stem either; it belongs to a viper flower. Don't you know that a woman picked a bunch of those and her tongue split in two? You're seven years old – when will you ever learn?

'Don't go near that field with your bare legs, poppy petals suck your blood; and don't step in that, you'll get your sabots dirty, little dung flower. Oh, don't put those shiny little black balls near your mouth: belladonna berries are a deadly poison. Who would have a daughter like you? Who's that in the distance, coming over the moor? We've not seen him before. And behind him, there, beside the small man, with its wheels in the air, I only hope that's not the Ankou's cart. Quick, Thunderflower, run and get me two needles!'

The mother spoke in a Celtic dialect and when she had finished, Thunderflower, little Hélène, so pretty with her blond hair spreading out like a dandelion, and scrawny feet beneath her violet skirt, galloped off, sabots and all, through a pool with rotting gorse and straw, towards a miserable farm with a roof of thatch, and dry-stone walls.

Stones! There was no shortage of those in this landscape. Everywhere the granite poked up through the holly and thistles. There were so many stones, with scant grass and such poor soil that the farming women spread wrack snatched from the sea on their land as fertiliser.

Two rows of menhirs, standing stones made of schist, sawed at the overcast sky. As the intruder drew closer, the moor seemed to bare its teeth showing gums of heather. Some river women came up from the wash place and joined the women working on the land to go up to Thunderflower's mother and ask, 'Who can that man be, coming towards us, Anne Jégado?'

'*War ma fé, heman ẓo eun Anko drouk.*' ('I would warrant that's an evil Ankou.') The gentleman was still approaching. He had a cane in his hand, a pipe in his mouth, new boots and a goatskin waistcoat. A gust of wind ruffled the few hairs on his forehead, which was creased in a frown.

'Hello there, ladies,' he called in French.

Visitors never came this way and the women and children watched him in astonishment, as he drew near, observing, 'The road that goes past your place is the worst imaginable. It crosses more than a hundred ponds and it's not wide enough for two vehicles to pass each other.' Smiling, he came closer still. As they waited for him, several of the women took out the pins that were holding the folds of their bodices together between their breasts.

'He won't be able to bring misfortune on any of us who can shed a drop of his blood.'

Close at hand now, the man introduced himself. 'My colleague over there and I are Norman wigmakers. We've come to buy hair in your region because even the men wear it long here.'

Facing him, the old women in their black dresses and the younger ones in reddish-brown skirts listened to him, stupefied, as if he were a traveller from exotic lands.

'Can you understand me?' the Norman said, worried by their disconcerted faces. 'Do you speak French, Mesdames?'

At that point, many of the women reached up to take out the needles securing the wings of their headdresses shaped like a horizontal figure of eight, which stuck out on either side of the head. The ends of the wide strips of white fabric tumbled on to their shoulders, and delightful Thunderflower, returning with little mud stockings, held out a needle to her mother, who had a plain flat headdress in everyday cloth. Meanwhile the wigmaker explained his presence.

'We landed on your shores this morning, and before we'd even gone three leagues our covered cart, which you can see behind me, slipped into a rut. Might there be some men in this village who could help us to get it—'

'*Ann diaoulou!*' yelled a female voice, whereupon all the washerwomen and farm women hurled themselves upon the Norman, brandishing their metal points. It was like a wasps' nest emptying on to his almost bald head. Suddenly surrounded, he was stuck with darts all over. The needles and pins went far into his thighs, back, legs, face and stomach.

'The Caqueux bleed from their navels!' 'The moon will swallow you up!' The savage Celtic cries surrounded the wigmaker, who shielded himself with his arms as his legs flailed wildly. People came swarming up from the banks and moors.

Lamenting his fate, the harvester of hair, understanding that he was suspected of bringing misfortune, uncovered his face to comment, 'You've hardly been touched by civilisation. Only here could one witness such superstitions.' A needle was thrust into one of his eyeballs. The wigmaker let out a yell. With his face in his hands he fled the circle of heathens, as a stout peasant woman chided, 'Oh, not in the eye! Who's put his eye out?'

The Norman ran off through pink heather and flowering buckwheat, that late summer's snow. ''Sdeath,' he shouted, and it was as if the women had thrown out Jesus Christ Himself. Once safely back with his horrified sidekick – a puny dark-haired man who moaned, 'Oh, that such a thing should be seen in the Empire of Napoleon' – the injured man turned round. With his good eye he could make out in the distance men at work breaking the moor, using picks to turn over the soil, which was so difficult and stony it would snap a ploughshare. These peasants would strive doggedly to get a few farthings out of the stones. But now, in their short waistcoats, wide breeches and round hats over long, flowing hair, their calloused hands on tools that looked straight out of the Middle Ages, they were doubled over with laughter.

At all the natives, both men and women, the maimed victim shouted, 'Fossils! Cretins! Degenerates!'

This took place in the hamlet of Kerhordevin in Plouhinec (Morbihan). The wigmakers unhitched the horse from their overturned cart with its yellow canvas. Anyone tilting their head sideways would have been able to make out the words 'À la bouclette normande: Normandy's finest tresses'. Bareback on their mount, they crossed a pond (where the steed went for a swim) still bawling, 'Idiots!' after the people they were leaving behind on the moor.

'*Piou ʒo aʒé?*' ('Who's there?')

The front door of a miserable cottage opened wide. Seated at her spinning wheel, Anne Jégado saw only the bright night and then the outline of her daughter appearing on the threshold.

'Oh, it's you, you naughty *groac'h* (sprite)! What a fright you gave me! Why did you knock three times before you came in?'

'I only banged my sabots to get the mud off them, Maman.'

'So you don't know, Thunderflower, that a chance noise repeated three times means misfortune? Don't you know that's what the Ankou does? Before he puts the body of a victim into his cart, he calls them three times in an eerie voice. For instance, for me he would call "Anne! Anne! Anne!" Look, your father was frightened as well. He immediately unsheathed his sword, messenger of misfortune. Where have you been at this hour, at *Penn ar Bed* (World's End)?'

'Leaning against a menhir on the moor.'

'Again? What can you be dreaming of, always leaning against those standing stones?'

Then, still in the *breȝhoneg* tongue, of course, since people at Plouhinec spoke only Breton, the mother demanded her daughter's sabots –'*Boutoù-koat!*'– so she could go and fill them with hot ash to dry and warm her little girl's feet.

In the hovel, filled with smoke from a fire fuelled with cowpats and dried turf, chestnuts were roasting under the ashes. A pot hanger and some pancake pans were suspended over a rusty trivet.

Thunderflower's father, sitting on one of the low walls on either side of the hearth, got up to put his sword back in its sheath above the fireplace. Its shiny blade was decorated with a coat of arms (gules a lion argent langued sable). One of his neighbours, a farm labourer, ensconced on the other side, rhapsodised, 'Oh, you're a true nobleman, Jean …'

'*Noblans Plouhinec, noblans netra!*' ('Nobility of Plouhinec, nobility of nothing!') said Jean Jégado, deprecatingly. 'Being descended from Jehan Jégado, the seigneur of Kerhollain, who saved Quimper when it was captured by the brigand La Fontenelle, doesn't make it any the less difficult for me to plough the moor today. But that's the fate of the younger sons of the aristocracy,' he conceded fatalistically, as he resumed his seat and took a Morlaix clay pipe out of his waistcoat.

Using his thumb, he filled it with poor-quality leaf tobacco, coarsely chopped. A brand at the end of a pair of tongs served as a match. Three puffs and a stream of saliva into the flames, then he lamented, 'Being the younger son of a younger son, himself born of a younger son who … At each inheritance the land is divided up in favour of the elder sons, so at the end of the line you find yourself with a tiny plot on this stony moorland. The year hasn't been great. If you have a bad harvest you can't pay for anything, so you sell what you have to pay your debts and the next thing you know, you're on the road, begging.'

The former nobleman had had to assume the fears of the poor peasants but maintained the pride of his lineage when with his wife, who was currently unpicking the hem of a pleated garment.

'Even though it seems that the stones of the Château de Kerhollain are soon to be sold off one by one, our arms are still at the top of the main window in the old church on the banks of the ria d'Étel. Alas, the window is so overgrown with moss that you can hardly see a thing any more. Some day I'll have to take a ladder and go and clean it with vinegar.'

Jean Jégado puffed away on the shaft of his short pipe, but the unsmokable tobacco would really have needed the breath of an air pump to get it going. He was the same age as his wife, around thirty, thin, with a chestnut-brown face, and clean-shaven but with very long hair. Jean was wearing the traditional *bragou-braz* (wide, knee-length breeches) and woollen stockings. He half opened his waistcoat, which fastened on the right with metal buttons.

'But enough of that. What have you got to tell us, Le Braz?' he asked the labourer sitting on the other side of the flames.

'Nothing,' replied the other man, his mind elsewhere. 'I was just thinking about your Hélène and her attraction to the standing stones.'

'Aren't you ever scared, all on your own on the moor at night?' Anne asked her daughter in amazement. She was sitting beside her on the chest seat against a box-bed, busy working on the hem.

'No, why?'

'When I was a little lad,' Le Braz recalled, 'people used to tell me that every hundred years the stones from the moor came to drink from the river and that during that time they gave up the treasures they were hiding …'

'Why, you silly girl? Because you might have run into the Ankou, for God's sake,' Thunderflower's mother fretted. 'You'd have asked him, "What are you doing here?" and he'd have replied, "I catch and I take." "Are you a thief then?" you'd have enquired, and he'd have admitted, "I am the one who strikes without fear or favour."'

'They told *me*,' put in Madeleine, Le Braz's wife, a round peasant woman with a face like a cider apple, who was spinning by hand beside the ploughman, 'that the standing stones were an army of motionless ghosts, a whole wedding party who'd been turned into stones for some mysterious misdeed.'

'Stand up,' Anne commanded her daughter, 'so I can check whether this dress fits you. Not even eight yet, Thunderflower, but see how you're growing!'

'Maman, who's this Ankou you're always talking about?'

The warmth of the fire was gradually loosening both limbs and tongues in the cottage with its floor of trodden earth and its barn separated from the humans by a waist-height partition. On the animals' side were a thin cow, three sheep, and a bald donkey, which shook its ears as Le Braz predicted, 'We'll be seeing fewer and fewer of the Druid stones here because when the clergy aren't using them as a quarry for building chapels, they're Catholicising them by carving Roman crosses at the top.'

Jean Jégado, resting the heels of his sabots on the sagging edge of a historic armchair spurned by his elders, was unsurprised.

'When religions succeed one another they merge. The new one gains the upper hand by swallowing up the old, and in time digests it.'

'The Ankou? He's Death's worker,' explained the mother,

16

holding the pleated skirt against the hips of her child, whose blond mop was filled with dust and as wiry as horsehair.

'Right, that'll still do fine for this year. Shift, so I can fold it and put it away.'

As she lifted the lid of the chest seat the mother revealed, 'There's nothing more frightening than the Ankou! He makes his way around Brittany with his cart and loads it up with the bodies of all those he strikes down, indiscriminately, as if by an invisible force.'

'What does he look like?' Thunderflower asked, suddenly greedy for information.

'But if one day there are no longer any menhirs, Anatole, what will the Poulpiquets go round ... brr, those nasty, hairy dwarfs that take you by the hand and drag you into a mad dance until you die of exhaustion?'

At a loss for an answer, Anatole Le Braz shook his head and demanded, '*Gwin-ardant!*' of his plump wife, who passed him a bottle of brandy, from which he poured a generous helping into an earthenware bowl for Jean Jégado as well.

'The Ankou wears a cloak and a broad hat,' said Anne Jégado, sitting down again. 'He always carries a scythe with a sharpened blade. He's often depicted as a skeleton whose head swivels constantly at the top of his spine like a sunflower on its stem so that with one glance he can take in the whole of the region his mission covers.'

'Have you seen him yourself, Maman?'

Once he had wiped his lips and filled his own and his host's bowl for a second time, Le Braz entered a world that was visible only to him: 'I saw a fairy the other day, or it might have been a

17

Mary Morgan. At any rate, it was a siren in a pond. She had come out on to a rock to bind her green hair while she sang. A soldier from Port-Louis was passing by and, attracted by her beauty and her voice, went up to her but the Mary Morgan put her arms round him and dragged him to the bottom of the pond.'

'Ah, fairies ...' said Madeleine. 'There are some very helpful ones, but others cause no end of harm.'

Jean, descendant of Jehan, his eyes glinting with the third *gwin-ardant*, downed in one, ventured to interrupt: 'Melusine, she's one thing, but Viviane le Fay, whoa, she leaves something to be desired.'

'No, of course I haven't seen the Ankou,' exclaimed Anne, raising her pale eyes to the ceiling. 'No one who sees the Ankou lives to tell the tale. But they say there's a statue of him in the cursed chapel belonging to the Caqueux — you know, those outcasts who live in the far-off moorlands. There's a standing stone over there as well, actually.'

'Why does the Ankou kill people?'

'Why? He doesn't need a reason, that Ankou, with his cart with the axle that's always squeaking. Squeak, squeak. He comes across people or finds a way into their homes, but never gets angry with anyone. He cuts them down, that's all. From house to house, that's his job, Death's worker.'

The child fell silent. In the evening, when people sat round together, the resin candle provided little illumination and the light would play tricks. The whistling of the wind outside was like the voice of a drowned man calling for a tomb. 'The sea has been making widows.' They had heard it too in the sound of the leaves. After brandy and a few bottles of bad cider, the imagination would get to dreaming here. Once the night grew very dark they would tell more than one tale that sent shivers down the spine. In the stifling, airless cottage, the swirls of fumes from the fireplace muddled the thoughts. 'I've seen a falling star. A priest's going to hang himself.'

From the outside, the wisps of smoke could be seen escaping in pale grey streamers beneath the door, from the edges of the little window, between the dry stones in the walls, and among the stalks of the thatch, then spiralling up towards the starry sky. Just as straw rotted in the pond, inside the hovel, minds were fermenting.

'I can hear a noise on the road!'

'Eh?'

'Didn't you hear a cart axle squeaking?' Anne asked the company.

'To be honest, no,' answered her husband.

'The noise! Horses panting so heavily you'd think it was a storm wind. The squeaking axle's going right through my head, yet you can't hear anything?'

'No,' said Anatole Le Braz.

'At one stage the carthorse began stamping on the spot as if it was stuck. How its hoofs beat the ground. It was like hammers on an anvil.'

Immediately everyone inside the cottage fell into a deep silence to listen properly. Jean's hair was standing on end so stiffly it looked to be made of needles. In the end Anatole got up to observe the road through the small window made of horn.

'Oh, it's the cart that overturned this morning! The two owners have come back with some men from the town and a second horse to get it upright again. They're holding lights around the covered cart.'

'They dare to come near our houses at night?' Jean was astounded.

'Particularly as they hardly got a friendly welcome in the daytime, especially the tall one in the goatskin waistcoat,' Madeleine Le Braz felt obliged to point out. 'I'd really love to know the name of whoever put his eye out.'

'How I didn't go mad, I don't know,' murmured Anne, still pale and trembling.

'Mad enough, to be sure,' her husband retorted in annoyance. 'Fancy getting into such a state over a cart being righted.'

'What *I* heard was no ordinary cart.'

'Oh, poor Anne, you're *briz-zod*.'

'No, I'm *not* stupid. You can shrug your shoulders all you like but I'm telling you, the Ankou's cart is going about in these parts. It won't be long before we know who he's coming for.'

Thunderflower's eyelids were fluttering like petals. 'It's time for you to say goodnight,' her mother pointed out.

While the child knelt up on the chest seat to open the panels of the box-bed, Jean Jégado asked offhand, just as if resuming a normal conversation, 'Le Braz, did you know that Cambry has turned into a black dog?'

'Jacques Cambry, who died last year? How do you know that?'

'He told me so himself. I met a black dog that said, "I am Cambry."'

The religion of the Druids, mother of tales and lies, left behind a phantom in Thunderflower's imagination as she slid on to a bale of oats big enough for three. She shooed away a hen so that she could pull up the coverlet made from scraps of material joined together, and laid her head on a sack of crushed gorse. Behind the doors she could hear other *nozve-ziou*, grown-ups' tales. The brandy stirred them into strange stories and confessions.

'Water sprites snatch away pregnant women!'

'The *bag-noz* is a siren-boat made of crystal, which takes its passengers to the isle from which no one returns.'

'Of course I joined the Chouans to fight for Louis XVI and the nobles! I was against the Great Revolution, that enemy of miracles.'

'Do you really not hear anything?'

Inside the box-bed, the child had caught a little golden scarab beetle crawling along against a board. Holding it close to one ear and tapping lightly with her nails again and again, Thunderflower listened to the cracking of the carapace, which sounded like the axle of the *karriguel an Ankou* squeaking as it started off: *squeak, squeak.*

Nyaaa, nyaaa . . .

In the distance, the drone of the biniou bagpipes, inflated by the player's breath, sounded a continuous note: *nyaaa*. Over this bass note, a reedy bombard gave the accompanying signal for the branle. The sounds of the instruments tore through the air. Men, women and children were dressed in their *fest-noz* costumes and, arm in arm, formed a Breton round dance. Clogs stamped in the mud and a voice began to sing: *'Canomp amouroustet Janet, Canomp amouroustet Jan!'* ('Sing we of the loves of Jeanne, sing we of the loves of Jean!') Thunderflower could see them all over there. The little bagpipe sounded an octave higher than the bombard. The notes had the tone of a man with a cold, and the *dohs* were *lahs*, but what did that matter? Hearing it brought a tear to the eye. 'Jean loved Jeanne, Jeanne loved Jean.'

In the middle of the circle of dancers, a large fire of branches, stuffed with firecrackers, had been lit. Explosions were shooting off in all directions, sending out stars sparkling into the darkness.

From Thunderflower's vantage point, the whirling pool of light looked like a small pancake on top of the moor, the more so since, when the sabots beating time came up, their soles took with them a yellow mud, which rose and stretched like a paste mixed with grit, the remains of the schist from the megaliths that used to be here but had recently been taken down and cut up to make lintels for church doors. Very soon, as if to return the compliment, the dancers would burn a crude wooden statue of the Virgin Mary on the pyre, and the crowd would fight over its charred remains.

'But since Jean has been Jeanne's husband, Jean no longer loves Jeanne nor Jeanne Jean!'

The song was at an end. The Mayor of Plouhinec stood up to speak, something that happened too often. Most of the company straggled off to the refreshment stall. Pancakes were piled up on the tables. The supply of *far* cake was replenished. The evening poured fire into the glasses at the feast and lads lit lanterns. A woman struck up a merry song, and the pipes and bombard joined in. Again, the thudding of heels was like heavy rain on the stone and the mud underfoot. The men's round hats bobbed up and down, with their two strips of black fabric fluttering at the back. The ribbons would part in the wind, one minute making the turning sails of a windmill, the next the rippling waves of the sea. Now, that was dancing!

A shepherdess, around ten years old, all dressed up, but whose finery could not disguise her plain, flat face, snub nose and bulging eyes, left the ring of torches to say to Thunderflower, 'Aren't you coming to the feast, Hélène? You seem to be in a dream.'

Hélène Jégado, the last descendant of her noble Breton family, was leaning against an enormous standing stone, which carried her thoughts up to the sky. On the moor drenched in moonlight, she felt the supernatural surrounding her. She took on the energy of the menhir and wallowed in the light and dark of the Breton legends. 'I hear again a distant, dying song.'

Thunderflower was wearing a white headdress, which came down over her ears. Opposite her, the little shepherdess held up her glass lantern so she could look at the Jégado girl, her sky-blue eyes so characteristic of the Celts.

'Hélène, why are you so near to the Caqueux' chapel? There's nothing here but evil spirits going about to trap the living. People say the chapel's where the fairies hold their deadly orgies and round this very standing stone is where the bearded dwarfs hide, the ones that appear and force you to join the dance until you die of exhaustion. You know, the ...'

'The Poulpiquets, Émilie.'

'I prefer dancing with the handsome lads at the *fest-noz*. Do you really not want to come?'

'No, I've got a date with the Ankou in the chapel.'

'What? First you venture into this cursed worship place, and now you say you're meeting Death's worker. Poor Hélène, you must be losing your mind.'

'Maybe ...'

Émilie stopped her ears so as not to hear any more. Lantern in hand, she ran back towards the feast while Thunderflower

23

slipped into the chapel. No sooner had she dipped her fingers not into holy water but into the sacred purificatory water of a pagan fountain than the child noticed the green wall paintings bulging out like the scales of some mythical creature. Their lacklustre colours were oppressive, and made the building's Romanesque vault seem to bear down on her. In that debased church, lit by a ray of moonlight coming through a window, it seemed that God had been defeated.

In front of the main window, enthroned on the altar, which contained an ossuary displaying skulls, was the statue of the Ankou. It was a skeleton holding a scythe taller than himself. Had someone read it to her, Thunderflower would have understood the inscription running round the thick edge of the granite table beneath the figure.

'I will spare no one. Neither pope nor cardinal will I spare. Not a king nor a queen. Nor their princes or princesses. I will spare neither priests, bourgeois, judges, doctors, shopkeepers nor, similarly, the beggars.'

There he is then, Death's worker, carved in black wood, the child thought, lifting her head. In place of eyes and nose, the Ankou had empty holes, and the lower jaw hung down. To the farmer's daughter, the curve of the blade the figure held seemed oddly positioned. The child felt an iciness penetrate the tranquillity of her body and her mind spun off in wild imaginings.

Outside, as Émilie the shepherdess ran across the moorland, her lantern cast a second, revolving beam of light through the window. It elongated the Ankou's shadow, which moved until it exactly merged with Thunderflower. Now the shadow of Death's worker appeared to be wearing a child's Breton headdress. The little girl's brain was sent mad by such a marvel. Just like the Ankou, she raised her arm as if holding a scythe.

'Why are there black balls in my *soupe aux herbes* and not in Hélène's?' Émilie wondered aloud as she took her place at the table next to Thunderflower, who was already seated. Anne Jégado, who was serving herself from the pot over the crackling logs, wheeled round in the cottage where the shepherdess had been invited to lunch at her daughter's request. The mother made her way towards the offending plate in astonishment.

'What black balls? Oh, those are belladonna berries. Don't eat them, whatever you do. Thank heavens you noticed them, little Le Mauguen! As for you, Thunderflower, what sort of joke is that you've played on Émilie? Haven't I told you these berries are poisonous? Thank goodness you didn't crush them first. You might have put far more in. We wouldn't have noticed a thing and then …'

Thunderflower wiped her mother's dripping brow as she lay flat on her back on the table. Then she gripped her hands tightly for a long while. 'You'll be all right, Maman.' The sick woman's eyes were vague and her breathing quickened. Violet blotches were coming out on her skin.

Le Braz, the neighbour, had come running. 'What's happened?' he asked.

'She went down like a cow with a hammer-blow to the head,' Jean Jégado answered. 'Hélène's described the scene for me. At

25

supper, Anne put out two plates of wheat gruel, for her and our daughter, then, while the youngster was eating, she went outside and blew the horn to call me in for the meal as well. When my wife returned she ate her gruel too; she criticised it for a bitter aftertaste but swallowed it all anyway, wiped her plate with some bread and that was it. Where's the ring she wore on her middle finger? It's a family signet ring with the Jégado crest engraved on it that I gave her on our wedding day.'

Madeleine Le Braz, ruled by Breton superstition, carried out the test of the ten candle ends, which she had cut to equal length. Five were placed on one side of the stricken woman, for death, five elsewhere, for life. The latter went out much sooner. 'The patient's had it,' the farm labourer's chubby wife predicted matter-of-factly.

'Is there someone coming?' asked Jean.

Anatole looked out of the cottage's one small window to check. 'No, why?'

'I thought I heard a cart jolting along.'

Madeleine was already strewing mint, rosemary and other aromatic leaves on the soon-to-be corpse. 'We also have to empty the water from the vases lest, at any moment, the dead woman's soul should drown there.'

Madame Le Braz executed this task while Jean, helpless and at a loss, not knowing how he could make himself useful, automatically reached for a broom handle.

'No, no *scubican anaoun* (sweeping of the dead)!' advised Madeleine. 'You never sweep the house of someone who's about to die because their soul is already walking around and the strokes from the broom might injure it.'

The farm cottage filled with sighs, though everyone was admiring of Thunderflower's zeal and devotion as, head bowed, she took such care of her sick mother, whose tongue was now green, flecks of foam hanging from her lips. Had they been able to see the small blonde girl's expression from underneath, however, they would have discovered something infernal about it. She was standing beside someone who was about to die ... It was like the birth of a vocation. As she put her little fingers to one of her genetrix's burning cheeks, it was like the child Mozart touching the keys of a harpsichord for the first time. She murmured something the adults took for a sob, '*Guin an ei ...*' ('The wheat is germinating ...') and her mother died, lowering only her right eyelid, which put Madame Le Braz in an instant panic: 'When a dead woman's left eye doesn't close it means someone else you know is in for it before long!'

'That's true, Hélène. You're right. The blade of the Ankou's scythe is fixed to the handle the opposite way round. But how do you know that at your age? In any case, the scythe belonging to Death's worker is different from those of other harvesters because its cutting edge faces outwards. The Ankou doesn't bring it back towards him when he cuts humans down. He thrusts the blade forward, and he sharpens it on a human bone.'

Her father demonstrated the gesture on the moorland, silver grey with lichens.

'Like that, well out in front. D'you see? But why are you concerned with that? Just as your big sister, Anna, is in service with the parish priest at Guern, you're about to go to join your godmother in the presbytery at Bubry, to work in abbé Riallan's household. You'll have to call him "Monsieur le recteur". What do you think you'll be scything over there?'

'Papa, are there people in Bubry?'

'Yes, it's quite a large village.'

'And is there belladonna there?'

'Of course. Why wouldn't there be?'

Hélène was biting greedily into a slice of bread when the dainty carriage belonging to a haughty gentleman arrived. He got out, exclaiming, 'Well now, Jégado the royalist, I expected to see you wearing blue. Aren't you in mourning?'

'In Lower Brittany, husbands never mark their widowhood, Monsieur Michelet. Only the animals on the farm observe mourning rituals. I put a black cloth over my hive and made my cow fast on the eve of my wife's funeral. You may as well learn that now, because you never know, you old revolutionary – who are soon to be married,' added Jean as he noticed the embroidery on the ribbons fluttering from the back of Michelet's hat, a sign that he was engaged.

The well-turned-out visitor – still young, square-shouldered, with a bearded jawline, and sporting a white leather belt and laced-up shoes – appraised Jean's two stony hectares, which stretched as far as the line of plum trees leading to the washing place.

'So you're selling your whole farm?'

'Even with Anne it was difficult. I'll never manage on my own. I'll leave you the cottage as it is, with contents. I'll just take my sword from above the fireplace.'

'What will become of you, nobleman?'

'Day labourer ... beggar ... I'll do what my neighbours do. You're well aware of the poverty and how many abandoned farms there are in the hamlet of Kerhordevin, since you're the one buying them all up.'

'How much do you want for yours?' asked the wealthy landowner.

'One hundred.'

'You must be joking! It's not the Jégado château at Kerhollain I'm getting. I'll give you fifty but, since I'm going through Bubry anyway, I'll drop your daughter at the priest's house as promised. That's a very pretty little fairy you've got there. How old is she?'

'She was baptised on 28 Prairial in year XI.'

'Year XI. Can't you say 1803? Are you still using the revolutionary calendar, Jean? Alas, that fine secular invention of the Great Revolution is over. An erstwhile Chouan like you should be rejoicing that we've gone back to the Christian calendar, the Gregorian one ...'

'Oh? I didn't know that. The only way those of us who can't read the papers have of hearing about important events is from songs at fairs, you see.'

'Go on, my little noblewoman, up you go into the carriage with your leather bag. It has a fleur-de-lis branded on it. Is it your father's? What have you got in it?'

'A cake I made.'

'Right. So, Jégado, you'll let me have your hovel?'

Pulling out a hair – the symbol of property – Jean threw it into the wind. This was the equivalent of signing a contract, declaring that you would not go back on the agreement, since it would be impossible for the seller to recover the hair, which the breeze had carried away.

The hair spiralled away in the wind, and the carriage, drawn by a mare, rolled off along a rutted road shaded by centuries-old oak trees. Putting her bag, which was divided into two sections, beside her, Thunderflower turned to watch her downcast father making his way back to the cottage. Soon the child lost sight of the Druid stones of her village as well.

Late afternoon. The bell was ringing for the angelus. The light, two-wheeled carriage came at walking speed past numerous flour mills and squat windmills and stopped in front of the presbytery in Bubry. The wealthy landowner was lying motionless on his side, with one arm hanging down. His discarded whip lay on the flour-scattered cobbles. Behind the presbytery gates a woman in servant's clothing and with bagnolet fluttering on her forehead called out, 'Monsieur le recteur! Monsieur le recteur!'

A priest came running to join the servant, who was wiping her hands on her apron and asking Thunderflower in Breton, 'What's the matter with him? He's got foam at his mouth and cake crumbs in his beard!'

'He's dead, Tante Hélène. It came over him just as we arrived in this street.'

'Oh, my poor little godchild, what a journey you must have had.'

The priest raised Michelet's head and gave his diagnosis in French. 'He must have had a heart attack.'

For the second time in her life, Hélène Jégado was hearing this strange language, of which she understood not one word.

'*Petra?*' ('What?')

She was looking now at the façade of the priest's residence, with carved coats of arms broken during the Revolution, while he was astonished by the sight of her blond mop of hair.

'Mademoiselle Liscouet, your late sister's daughter goes bare-headed?'

'Girls don't wear a headdress except at *fest-noz* until they're thirteen, abbé Riallan,' his servant reminded him.

'What do you enjoy doing?' the clergyman asked the girl in *brezhoneg*.

'Cooking, Monsieur le recteur.'

'Fine, then you'll help your godmother peel the vegetables, wash up, put the stores away in the outbuilding, and learn French. Give me your bag. Goodness, the man who brought you here lost not only his life but one of his shoelaces as well.'

Bubry

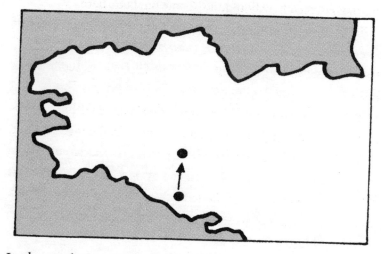

In the presbytery kitchen, Thunderflower was having her hair done by her godmother. Standing opposite a piece of broken mirror fixed to the door, the Jégado girl glanced at her reflection from time to time. Behind her back she could see her mother's sister smoothing her long blond hair out towards the top of her head and rolling it into a chignon, and then she felt hairpins sliding in against her scalp.

The niece gave a hasty glance to the right. She asked for a pause before her aunt should go on to the next phase of the hairdressing, just long enough for her to go and dip a ladle into the saucepan and blow on the surface of the broth to drive the gathering froth to the edges.

'You must always remove it as it forms. You were the one who taught me that, Godmother, as well as the correct way to brown butter. Will you teach me lots of other things?'

'A good cook never gives away all her little secrets,' smiled her maternal aunt, who was dressed in a Lorient apron with a large bib that covered her shoulders. 'Come on, back here.'

Once back in position in front of the door with the piece of broken mirror, Thunderflower passed a significant milestone: a Breton headdress was positioned on top of her chignon. It was just a simple square of white tulle, as befitted a domestic, but it was edged with lace. Her godmother explained how it was arranged, folding it here, turning it up there, in the local manner.

'Each district has its own kinds of embroidery and folds. There we are, now everyone can see you're a grown-up girl. Just look at you with your mane neatly tamed at last. Wouldn't anyone think you were an angel fit to receive Holy Communion without the need for confession first?'

Thunderflower burst out laughing, caught in a ray of sunlight that lit up a sideboard, and she saw her reflection swing round as the abbé Riallan opened the door and came into the kitchen, asking, 'Who would you give Holy Communion to, Mademoiselle Liscouet?'

'Why, my goddaughter, of course. We can only congratulate ourselves on her.'

The priest of Bubry noticed the headdress. 'Are you thirteen already then?'

'This very day, 16 June!' exclaimed her godmother.

'That calls for a celebration,' said the gentle, elderly priest. 'I was about to leave for Pontivy to meet the abbé Lorho, who will be replacing me soon. Would you like to come with me, Hélène? While I'm at the church you could buy some goodies, as it's your birthday, and also whatever we need to sort out the rat problem in the outbuilding before my successor gets here.'

'Of course, with pleasure, *aotrou beleg*.'

'Monsieur le curé,' the clergyman corrected the girl.

'Oh, yes, sorry … Of course, Monsieur le curé.'

With that she undid the ties on her apron while the man of the Church heaped praise on her.

'That's all right. The French language will come. Still a few Bretonisms sometimes, but you're making excellent progress.'

Once outside the presbytery gates, while a stable boy was harnessing a clapped-out pony to the cart into which the priest clambered with some difficulty, Thunderflower had a good look at the village of Bubry, a higgledy-piggledy collection of houses with water troughs, a firewood seller and, above all, mills. Near the market where meat was sold, a butcher reminded Riallan he should send someone for what was due to him: '… because when an ox or pig is slaughtered the head is kept for Monsieur le curé.' Hélène was just lifting her buckled shoe on to the running board when she stood back down, most astonished to see, across from her on the other side of the road, the two Norman wigmakers who had overturned their cart in a rut one day at Plouhinec.

In front of the torn yellow cover, and beneath the lettering 'À la bouclette normande', the short wigmaker was setting out chairs and getting scissors ready while the taller one – almost bald, with a black band over his left eye – was clapping his hands, calling to people, 'Five sous per head of hair! Who wants to earn five sous in exchange for their hair?'

Beside the wall where the Normans were making their preparations, there stood three posts with rusty iron chains hanging from them. Workmen covered in flour were coming out of a mill for their lunchtime break. They had long hair touching their shoulders and covering their eyes. They kept pushing their long locks behind their ears, creating a cloud of dust, while the wigmaker tried to sound conciliatory.

'Even though we'd prefer it neat and washed, there's no problem, good sirs. We'll still buy your hair as it is. Take a seat.'

But it was the three posts the workers were making for, each mortifying himself as he went: 'How I regret my wicked deed! I should never have done that! Oh, I've done such a bad thing, I'm so angry with myself!' They leant their foreheads against the posts and wound locks of their hair through the rings, all the while reproaching themselves: 'I said nasty things to my mother! I robbed my brother! I betrayed my neighbour!' Then they yanked their heads violently backwards, tearing out their hair, which came away together with the scalp. On the ground traces of blood and skin could be seen, to the stupefaction of the two Norman wigmakers, who were hopping up and down now.

'What are you doing? You're mad! What savagery! That's unbelievable! Where on earth are we? If you think we're going to pay five sous for raggy bits of scalp …'

The Normans were shouting so loudly that their surprised horse instinctively kicked out its back hoofs, catching the weedy wigmaker – who had just gone between the shafts to fetch a basin hanging on the front of the cart – full in the jaw and breaking one of his shoulders as well. The tall, one-eyed man snatched up his colleague and bundled him under the yellow canvas, then, abandoning the chairs, leapt on to the vehicle seat and whipped the horse, which galloped off northwards. Reins in hand, he turned and yelled at the self-torturing Bas-Bretons, 'Sickos! Nutters!'

The inside of the pharmacy at Pontivy resembled a sacristy in hell – smocked employees speaking in hushed voices, jars labelled in Latin, mysterious little packets. The man in charge of the establishment, who wore a monocle, asked, 'Who's next? You, pretty maid? What would you like?'

'*Reusenic'h.*'

'What?'

'*Reusenic'h!*'

'Oh, arsenic.'

'Yes, for killing rats. The priest at the presbytery in Bubry where I work in the kitchen told me to buy some while he went to his meeting.'

The pharmacist turned round, then proffered a minuscule bottle.

'That's light,' Thunderflower said, weighing it in her hand.

'Ten grammes, but it's to be used with the greatest of care,' admonished the man of science as he took the servant's money. 'This substance is very dangerous.'

'But not as dangerous as belladonna.'

'Oh, much more so, my dear,' he said, handing her the change. 'The doses must be infinitesimal. Be very careful, won't you? Don't go using it for pastries just because you're from Bubry. It may look like flour, but it's not the same at all.'

'*Kenavo.*'

*

Just as Thunderflower was pulling open an oven door, the abbé Riallan pushed open the kitchen one, and came in, scratching his tonsure.

'Hélène, I'm telling you this as truthfully as I would say the angelus: I do not understand. Since you put that white powder in the outhouse, the rats there have been getting fatter and fatter and their numbers are increasing.'

'Oh?' answered the adolescent, carefully placing a burning hot tray on the clay tiles.

'I saw one the size of a cat against the grain chest. They're swallowing the product from the chemist's, which is supposed to exterminate them, yet it's as if they were stuffing themselves without suffering any harm. Is there any of it left? I'd like to try again.'

'No, I've emptied the bottle,' said Thunderflower, sliding a spatula under one of the little cakes on the tray and putting it onto a dish.

'When your aunt comes back from the market, please ask her to come and see me at the church. Oh dear, dear, whatever will the abbé Lorho think of me?' worried the rector, pushing open the glass door to the courtyard, just before Hélène's godmother came in by the other door, carrying baskets and sniffing.

'Mmm, there's a lovely smell of caramelised crust in here.'

Her goddaughter, carefully washing a bowl and a spoon, told her, 'While you were out, I tried to invent a cake. Monsieur le recteur would like to speak to you.'

'Let's taste your speciality first.'

The niece advised her aunt to blow on it because it was hot. 'Since I was able to buy some, thanks to the priest giving me money for my birthday, I've put crystallised angelica in it.'

'That's very kind.'

Putting the small round caramelised cake between her lips, Hélène Liscouet bit into it and began to chew. Her face flushed, there was instant dryness of the mouth and mucus membranes, and she was gripped by a raging thirst.

'Something to drink!'

Weakness of the muscles and dizziness followed, and then she could no longer stand, and her legs gave way beneath her.

Séglien

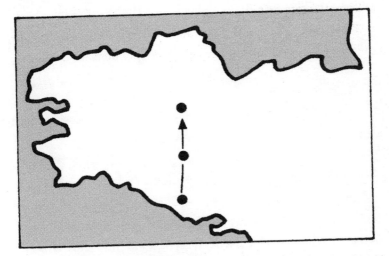

'So the priest at Bubry didn't call the doctor immediately, then?' a servant, hands on her hips, asked Thunderflower, who was leaning on her elbows at the table in a different kitchen.

'Yes, he did, Tante Marie-Jeanne. But when he reached the bed where Godmother was thrashing about like a mad thing, he just put some dust into a box. He drew a cross in it and said, "In the name of the Father," adding, "The patient will be cured if she gives a few sous to Saint Widebote." I've kept the last towel she wiped her lips on as a memento.'

In pride of place on the table stood a loaf of rye bread beside a sickle-shaped knife. Thunderflower ran her finger lovingly along the blade as her second maternal aunt lamented, 'You poor girl.

Both my sisters: your mother, then your godmother.'

'What's more,' complained Thunderflower, 'I'd just baked a little cake I'd invented for her. I couldn't even find out whether she liked it. I'd intended one for the abbé Riallan too, but with all the fuss I forgot to serve it to him. I've brought it in my bag – would you like to try it?'

'Have you put ground almonds in it?'

'They're in there too.'

'Oh, yes, you're right, Mother. At eighteen, Hélène is quite magnificent! She'll turn a few heads, that one, and in my opinion it won't be long before she finds a young man.'

The priest of Séglien, a real gentleman who was surely very popular with his parishioners, was seated in the depths of an armchair across from his mother, who was sipping her lime tisane. On the low table between them stood little cups of plums in syrup, newly brought by Thunderflower. As his very pretty servant left the drawing room for the kitchen, the clergyman turned to watch.

'Did I tell you, Mother, that her aunt Marie-Jeanne, who was in my employ for many years, dropped dead the very day her niece arrived to see her, following a death in their family?'

'I didn't know that.'

'Is it really that long since you've ventured outside the walls of Saint-Malo to visit your son, lost among the savages of Basse-Bretagne, you heartless mother?' the priest joked.

'Since I was widowed I don't travel much, and it's a long journey here on such rough roads that you fear death with every turn of the wheel. What did Marie-Jeanne die of? Your father always said that fatal dysentery was rife in the area where you serve.'

'That's right. Lots of people also suffer attacks of virulent skin diseases. In any case, since Hélène had already worked in a kitchen and was talented, I entrusted her with her aunt's job and I'm very satisfied with her. A kind heart, dedicated to her work, clean, and she gets on like a house on fire with my maid.'

The priest's mother said approvingly, 'Your father always said that, these days, finding a cook of the right calibre ...'

Thunderflower returned with a plate of biscuits, which she put down, then, turning round, exclaimed in tones of mock-disgust, 'Oh, look, there on the carpet behind you, mouse droppings. Monsieur l'abbé, we'll have to buy something to kill rats. I was just thinking that, since your mother's here, I could take this opportunity to go to the pharmacy at Pontivy.'

The abbé Conan leant down to pick up what his cook had pointed out. 'Those aren't rodent droppings, they're coffee beans. Just now, when you were using a hammer to grind beans wrapped in a cloth, some must have escaped and rolled on to the carpet. I'd have been very surprised in any case, since I've had the place cleared of rats.'

Hélène gave a forced smile at being thwarted.

'Have a rest now, Hélène,' the good priest suggested. 'You could even stay here with us and draw – you like that – instead of mouldering alone in your room.'

Madame Conan considered her son's attentions to be a little too progressive. With a Breton *sablé* crumbling in her teeth, she murmured, 'Your father always used to remind us "To each his own place ..." Having said that, it *is* sad to lose an aunt so suddenly.'

Thunderflower – strong and wholesome as bread and water, and statuesque, by God; to see her was to love her – was now seated elegantly at a card table, drawing swirls on a sheet of paper. 'Perhaps Tante Marie was *goestled*,' she surmised.

'Hélène means "dedicated",' the rector of Séglien translated for his mother. 'In this region, when someone dies of an unexplained illness, people declare, "He or she's been dedicated to Notre-Dame-de-la-Haine."'

'Notre what?' choked the widow, her mouth full of another biscuit.

'Have a little more tea to help it down. You see, Mother, before they were forced to convert to Catholicism, the Bretons here had altars dedicated to the death of others, and they've been determined to keep this cult going, as at Trédarzec, for example. Over there, Saint-Yves chapel was rebaptised Our-Lady-of-Hatred. People pray to Santez Anna, ostensibly the grandmother of Christ, but in actual fact Deva Ana, the grandmother of some Celtic gods – I think that's it. People go by night to the oratory to pray for someone's death.'

Madame Conan was stupefied. 'And the Roman Catholic Church puts up with these outlandish practices within those walls?'

Thunderflower, all this while, was drawing drowning angels.

'Of course not,' her son replied. 'The rector of Trédarzec is determined to have the chapel torn down and the statue of Santez Anna turned into firewood.'

'Your father was so right when he used to say, "The language that the Bas-Bretons have preserved, and their scorn for that of the French, is not conducive to the spread of new ideas in this region."'

Scoring out the smudged wings of an angel lost amid the swirls, Thunderflower asked, 'Where's Trédarzec?'

'Not very far from here, across from Tréguier,' answered the priest.

'In Morbihan?'

'No, in Côtes-du-Nord, near the reefs in the Channel where the wreckers wait.'

'The wreckers?'

Trédarzec

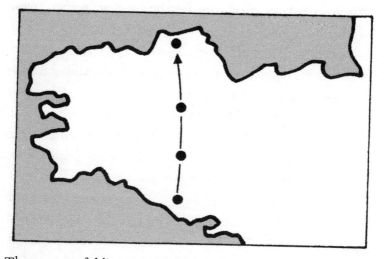

The sun was folding away its fan and a few birds hovered high in the skies. The evening lengthened Thunderflower's shadow as she stood by the edge of a coastal river in Tréguier, watching the village of Trédarzec on the opposite bank. Her father's double-bag on her left shoulder, one part hanging in front, the other down her back, she spotted the oratory of Notre-Dame-de-la-Haine at the top of the hill. Several winding paths led to it across the gorse and heather. Soon, near a stone bridge spanning seaweed left stranded by the low tide, Hélène Jégado was overtaken by other human shadows. Ashamed, they slipped, heads bent, along the paths leading to the mysterious chapel. As darkness fell, more people approached the building. Bigoudènes, with their slanted eyes and prominent cheekbones like Mongolian women, came forward like black birds, followed by workers and shopkeepers from Tréguier, who were whispering to one another, 'Look, over there, that woman who appears to have gone into a decline, Rondel has dedicated her. It's only a matter of time now.'

They walked on, their bare feet burning on nettle leaves. Thunderflower followed them to where an instinct was guiding her. At the top of the hill, bare of greenery, she bent her head to slip under a doorway, and stood up inside the chapel whose beams were festooned with spider webs.

On the altar cloth stood the statue of Our-Lady-of-Hatred. It was actually a classic Virgin Mary, with wavy hair falling along her arms and hands folded, but her face had been given lots of wrinkles and her body was painted black with a white skeleton over it. At the time she was moulded, this plaster Mary had doubtless been very far from imagining that she would one day be travestied to this extent and venerated to the accompaniment of prayers as un-Catholic as the ones being addressed to her here.

'Notre-Dame-de-la-Haine, grant that my brother may soon be lying in his coffin.'

'I ask you for the death of my faithless debtors.'

All round Thunderflower, souls full of rancour were very softly invoking the so-called grandmother of Christ, asking her to grant them the death of an enemy or a jealous husband within a year.

'I want him to croak within this strict time limit.'

Some were in a hurry to inherit: 'My parents have lived long enough.'

Three Hail Marys piously repeated and the people were

ready to believe in the power of prayers offered in this church dedicated to the cult of death. The girl from Plouhinec was just thinking to herself that some fine dramas were underway around her when on her right she heard a man's gravelly voice: 'Our-Lady-of-Hatred, send me a shipwreck.'

Thunderflower swivelled her head towards a fellow of about twenty-five, his complexion suggesting he was used to the rocking of the wind and the waves, who finished his prayer and left.

She followed him outside and asked: 'What's your name?'

'Yann Viltansoù. What's yours?'

It was his turn to look at her. Thunderflower's absolute perfection had something about it that froze him in his tracks. The extreme charm she exuded captured Viltansoù's heart instantly. 'Have we seen each other in our dreams?' he asked.

'How heavily you're breathing,' she said.

'That's because it's hot,' he replied, in the cold night.

'Gulls, gulls, bring our husbands and our lovers home to us ...'

The following afternoon, along a beach made of white sand and broken shells that looked like crushed bones, Yann Viltansoù was passing the time by singing the song of the sailors' companions under his breath: 'Gulls, gulls ...'

Thunderflower, her dainty black buckled shoes in one hand, was walking barefoot alongside the former stable boy, who had had enough 'of bedding down in the horses' manger to look after the animals'.

Now dressed in seaman's clothing from several countries —

baggy breeches like an English explorer, a red belt like a Spanish fisherman, a Dutch trader's tarred hat – he bent down to show the girl from Plouhinec how to gather razor clams, known here as 'knife handles'.

'When the tide is out, you sprinkle salt on the sand. The creature thinks the tide's coming in. It wriggles up to the surface, and you grab it. I've also found you two river pearls.'

'Thank you.'

Thunderflower, gazing out to sea lost in thought, felt an overwhelming emptiness inside her. The sight of this sterile infinity brought her to tears. Over there, the islands looked like sleeping whales and nearer to the shoreline, richly coloured rocky islets were like jewels set in the silvered foam of the waves. When the waves were high, shafts of light criss-crossed them in shimmering ripples, and cormorants glided into the bed of the wind. Their pulley-like cry was an answer to Yann's secret concern: 'Will we catch any game from the sea tonight?'

Some men came towards Viltansoù, who raised his hand to his hat in greeting. One had a bare torso reminiscent of one of those wooden logs the sea throws up on the beach. A tall, bald individual, an incongruous mixture of eunuch and slaughterman, was conversing with an old man with lots of white curls about the way to save a drowning man.

'Might as well save their breath,' moaned Yann, examining the sea through his spyglass.

The waves took on a violet colour where there was seaweed underneath the surface. There was now a mixture of reflections and shifting light. In the distance, the boats went by, their sails furtively bleeding in the light of the setting sun. Some women arrived on donkeys. On the customs men's path, bordered by thistles and brambles, a cow was grazing the granite. A wise woman foretold the future from the dance of the waters. Men knelt at the sight of the star of Venus. They were dressed in *berlinge*, a fabric of wool and hemp, out of which they made their yellowish brown waistcoats and breeches. Viltansoù observed the movement of ships in the distance, and noted sudden changes in the atmosphere. The noise of thunder shook the air. It grew suddenly dark and the wind whipped up the sea. Lightning flashed a zigzag course, and a bolt struck the coast.

By now, sky and sea were indistinguishable. Yann smiled, seeing the vessels suddenly headed for disaster. 'Come to me!' he told them. 'It's a game.'

Leaving the sand to climb back up to the coastal path that skirted the edge of the cliff, Viltansoù, with Thunderflower in his wake, hung a heavy copper and glass signal lamp between the horns of the waiting cow. Lighting it, he explained to the girl from Plouhinec, 'I'm burning coal because when the weather's bad, full of rain and fog, it gives a brighter light than oil burners, which get dull and are less visible on the horizon.'

Faced with the puzzled look of this splendid woman from Morbihan, who seemed not quite to understand what was going on, Yann from Côtes-du-Nord said by way of justification: 'A ducal prerogative has given us the *droit de bris*, permission to help ourselves from wrecks washed up on the shore. But since natural shipwrecks beside the coast are fairly rare, we have to help destiny along a bit. Long live organised fate, and shoo!' he cried to the cow, which began to move, notwithstanding the weight of the gleaming lantern bowing its neck.

While the bovine hoofs trampled the stones, Thunderflower recalled, 'Round the dunes where I'm from, when we want to find the body of someone who's drowned, we put a lighted candle on top of a loaf and set it adrift on the water. The corpse is found beneath the place where the loaf stops.'

Viltansoù was mocking. 'If we did that here the shore would be one big bakery.'

The wind blew the flame and harried the glass in the lantern. The sea grew increasingly angry. Yann was watching it from the top of a rock.

'There! Over there! A boat's coming! Get the cow going! Oh, I did the right thing yesterday, going to pray to Our-Lady-of-Hatred!'

The bovine lighthouse made its way along the coast. The non-stop swaying of its head sent shimmering waves of light back and forth at regular intervals across the water. On board the vessel, the crew were deceived by the light, which they believed they could follow. It was the weather for a tragedy; shipwrecks seemed to be written in the stars. The former stable boy called to the ship, 'This way! Come! The way is clear and it ends in your death.'

Beneath her soaking wet headdress trimmed with lace, Thunderflower was licking her lips. The ocean was huge and fearsome, forming peaks and troughs, sometimes deep as the grave. The waters were raging so uncontrollably that it was as if the poles had lost their magnets. Viltansoù who, spyglass to his eye, could make out the vain efforts of the sailors on the bridge, gave precise information regarding the time and place of the collision.

'Ten minutes from now, on the Maiden's Teeth rocks.'

And indeed, the ship was drifting towards the reef, with no hope of avoiding disaster.

'Everyone must perish,' said Yann.

'Yes, oh, yes,' sighed the girl from Plouhinec.

Beneath the cliffs, the locals ran to hide behind the rocks across from the reefs indicated by Yann. Armed with hooked poles and ropes, they crouched down to wait, their eyes fixed on the dark waters and the sea's gifts with rapacious greed. Suddenly there was an enormous crack right in front of them, and splinters of boards flew about. On the Maiden's Teeth, a series of rocks where seaweed rotted, the ship had impaled itself as on a knife blade, which had sliced it like a fruit. And indeed, hundreds of thousands of oranges came tumbling from the gaping bow. Rushing towards the broken vessel came crowds of women and children with bags and baskets. Like a horn of plenty, the wreck was spreading a flotsam of luminous exotic fruit. Thunderflower came down quickly and filled her turned-up apron several times, making a pile all to herself on the sand. A wealthy trader from Saint-Brieuc, who owned the ship, had fallen overboard and was drowning, shouting for help in Breton: '*Va Doué, va sicouret!*' ('My God, help me!')

'Of course we will. That's what we've come for,' guffawed the old man with the full white locks, beside the slaughterman with the face of a eunuch, who thought it perfectly fair to go and disembowel the trader and grab his belt, doubtless stuffed with gold coins.

Driven on by the demon of pillage, the coastal peasants hurled themselves furiously on the remains of the ship. They clubbed down the wretched survivors who were stretching out their arms to them for help, stripped them, and mocked the drowned ship's boys who had been at table in the hold below.

'Whatever can have made those children so ill?'

'They'd just eaten their bacon soup.'

'Maybe there was something wrong with the meat.'

Many of the sailors were thrown into the sea, sinking to the depths of a pitiless grave that instantly forgot their names. At the bottom of this natural abyss, the rocks were turning red. The play of the mists and foam made them appear to be moving. The women also climbed aboard port and starboard. They exuded a mad sexuality, clambering up phallic ropes wearing no undergarments, their skirts hoicked up on their bare thighs. Even bolder and more fearless than the men, they reached the height of cruelty with the last survivors, forcing themselves on them.

'Go on, take me, that'll be a change from a cabin boy's arse. And don't say no, or else guess where the hook of my stick'll be going.'

On the bridge, their cuckolded husbands were getting drunk. When they had consumed their fill of wines and brandy, they downed a whole chest of medicines, which killed some and sent the others into convulsions. The sky was filled with an apocalyptic tangle of cries. On the beach, Thunderflower witnessed all this without getting involved. It's not my area of expertise, she thought. But she watched with relish as a bottle that had escaped from the wreck floated towards her, and she grasped hold of it. How well arranged life is: on the litre bottle filled with white powder, the girl from Plouhinec recognised the label, which was like the one on the tiny vial bought in the pharmacy at Pontivy. As Viltansoù came back on to the sand with his arms full of boxes, she asked, 'Can you read, Yann? What's written on here?'

'There? Arsenic.'

'*Reusenic'h?* Why were they travelling with that?'

'In the bowels of a ship, what people fear most is rabbits or rats, which could gnaw at the wood of the holds and sink them in the middle of the ocean. And that *would* be a shame – for us! Come on, throw that useless thing away and come and help yourself from the wreck as well.'

Thunderflower placed the bottle upright snugly between her lovely rounded breasts.

'I've got *my* trophy already.'

Then as Viltansoù, raising his eyes, neared her pile of oranges on his way back to the ship, she put her order in as if he were going to the grocer's: 'If there's any sugar, bring me some.'

Thunderflower was making jam. On the previous evening, Yann had found sugar (brown, to the Morbihan woman's amazement) and had also brought back a cask of rum – an alcohol of whose existence Hélène Jégado had been unaware. She poured a little of it over the deseeded citrus fruit quarters and the zest, boiling in cane sugar and water.

It was inside Viltansoù's curious dwelling that she was stirring away with a wooden spoon amid the sugary fragrances, and singing in shrill tones. In actual fact the house was the upturned back half of the hull of an inshore fishing boat, which had been wrecked one night, sheared across as if by a razor on the Witch's Fangs archipelago.

Once pulled with ropes to the top of a dune, the upturned

hold of the old tub henceforth formed the curved roof of a most individual home. Daylight came in through the portholes. Yann had covered up the open part of the wreck with boards from another vessel's bridge, placed upright. Then he had cut an opening to put in the mahogany door from a captain's cabin. There it was, squeaking as Viltansoù came in through it.

There was no floor at Yann's. When it rained, the ground ran with water. For this reason he had not put a sailor's mattress on the ground. He had preferred to extend the triangular sail of a fishing boat horizontally in the air like a hammock. Through the eyelets in the three corners of the jib, he had stretched ropes to three places in the shelter. Viltansoù's eyes went from the sail to the girl from Plouhinec, who was pouring her orange jam into jars, turning them over as soon as they were closed.

'You can taste it in a moment.'

'No, it's only you I'm hungry for.'

While the jam was cooling, Thunderflower's lover was growing hotter. 'The seductive power you exert is so sudden and so commanding. The enchantment of your smile is even more disturbing. A pollen of sensuality floats around you. You perfume the air.'

Goodness, the wrecker was growing sentimental. He went on, 'Your eyes are like blue flowers in milk' and that kind of nonsense, before suggesting: 'You know, we'd be comfortable, just the two of us, hidden in that sail.'

All the furnishings here had been looted in various shipwrecks: a whalebone crucifix was nailed up beside a clock whose glass was broken, above an anchor with its rope for decoration. The portrait of a stern Irish sea captain, complete with a hole made by a hooked pole, appeared to be making a disapproving face. Was it because, across from him, the sail was beginning to move without his orders? The white sail rocked as the entwined lovers tumbled like pebbles on the shore. One moment it wrapped them round completely like a cocoon, the next it unfolded, and grew taut, tossing them up into the air. The girl from Morbihan lobbed her cook's headdress, her hairpins and her dress over her head. She straddled Viltansoù's bare hips as he lay on his back, her long wavy blond hair tumbling down to the points of her breasts. The wrecker cupped them in his killer's hands. This girl was his favourite shape. With her pert bust, she danced, seated on him, moving her navel, and his eyes went spinning with delight.

As Yann's gaze became more vacant, she began to sway, casting the flying net of her caresses around the young man, who turned her on to her knees. She: arms stretched wide apart, holding on to the eyelets of the tack and sheet as her guitar-shaped bottom burst into melodies. He: clinging to Thunderflower's sides. Into the swing of things now, she moved her hips from right to left, backwards and forwards, then Viltansoù began to cry out Jesus's name again and again.

'Will you try my orange jam, Yann? There's a secret ingredient in it.'

'I don't eat jam.'

The dawn mist was licking itself like a she-cat emerging from its dreams when Viltansoù woke up. He patted the area around him with his hands, and was surprised not to feel anyone there. Sitting on the edge of the hanging sail, he noticed that his marine anchor

54

had disappeared as well, and that the door of his half-hull house was standing wide open. As he finished dressing among the reeds of a dune at the foot of a high escarpment that summer morning, he noted that little remained of the vessel loaded with citrus fruit, guided to its destruction two evenings before. Almost everything had been looted, carried away: cargo, furnishings, portholes, sails for making into rainproof garments or covers, and practically all the wood, which would serve for heating or building. The ship that, in the storm, had sought the port of Saint-Brieuc was now nothing but a washed-up fish skeleton.

Viltansoù heard someone calling him from near the wreck: 'Are you coming?' It was Thunderflower, sitting naked on the furthest rock of the Maiden's Teeth. Yann was concerned for her.

'Be careful you don't topple over. There's a huge abyss behind you.'

'Come …'

On the cliff top, the two Norman wigmakers were walking along the coastal path in front of their horse, holding its reins to get the covered cart to go between the spiny thickets. The shorter of the two griped, 'You can shay what you like, but I'm telling you that the reputation of Breton bone fixersh is vashtly overeshtimated. You can't tell me it'sh normal to have a shoulder like thish.'

'But the healer promised it would sort itself out.'

'Yearsh later? Look, he'sh put my arm back the wrong way round.'

It was true that the joints of the limb formed unusual angles.

'And it'sh not at all practical for cutting hair.'

The speech defect resulted from the hoof kick to his jaw

received at Bubry, which had been equally badly set.

'It'sh annoying me. Would it be all right with you if we untied the horshe and I had a little resht?'

'Ash you wish,' joked his tall colleague with the one eye.

Thunderflower spotted the two Normans unharnessing their outfit up above, then looked down to watch Viltansoù coming towards her. He jumped from one rock to another, approaching her in the same way one falls in love, aware it is a risky journey.

'You madcap, the men who associate with you will soon lose their way. Ah, you're leading me a merry dance, you enchantress.'

'Come …'

He was helpless to resist the call of the nymph, seated gracefully, legs crossed to one side. The reflections of the light on the waters played along her ankles and calves, more than knee-deep in the sea, drawing scales on them, while her feet, heels together but toes apart, looked like a fishtail.

'Goodnessh, a shiren.' Thus the portly wigmaker, with his arm making the shape of a figure five above the cliff as he pointed.

'A siren? You poor thing, you're becoming more and more Breton since that hoof-kick in the head,' moaned the one-eyed man, turning towards the sea.

Down below on the rocks, surrounded by the mirrors and chandeliers of the waves, Thunderflower held out her hand to her lover, singing in an unearthly voice, 'Come …' In her slow, clear voice there crept a serpent, like the rope that, as a joke no doubt, the woman from Morbihan was winding round Yann's neck. Then, behind her back, she gave a push to the anchor she had stolen from him. Viltansoù swayed, 'Aaaargh,' before plummeting head first to the bottom of the abyss. Large bubbles burst on the water's surface; the tall wigmaker was dumbstruck. Thinking he must be seeing things, he rubbed his good eye. 'That can't be happening. It's just not possible.'

'Ha, Monsieur Viltansoù didn't like jam.'

On her rock, Thunderflower resumed the pose of a mermaid dwelling in the sea.

Her lovely eyes were languid – beautiful, sad, the last of her line – as she ran her fingers like a comb's teeth through her sunbeam hair.

'No, it can't be real.' The one-eyed man couldn't believe what he saw. 'Sirens don't exist!' He raised his hand and brought it down hard, unfortunately on the horse's rump. It kicked its hind legs in the air. The short wigmaker was relieved to be standing by the beast's nostrils but, as it brought its hoofs down on the ground again, the horse slipped on the cliff edge. It tried to save itself with its forelegs, only in the end to topple backwards in a shower of pebbles. The tall Norman, seeing their horse skinned and already rotting, white among the rocks, yelled out, 'I'm growing heartily sick of Brittany!'

Guern

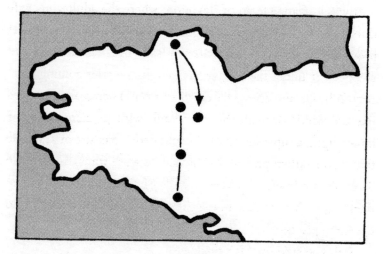

In the church, death flitted among hideous grotesques and bizarre, mocking faces, and paintings depicting tears and agonies, thorns and nails hung all around. Cries could also be heard.

'If you don't take my child's fever away, I'll whip you like a mule!'

'Heal me, or watch out for a beating!'

'Here, take that!'

In a wall niche stood the polychrome plaster figure of a Breton saint who, when he failed to answer prayers, was roundly whipped.

'Saint-Yves-de-Vérité, during your lifetime you were just. Show that you still are, by God!'

'The profits of my shop are almost nil. It's in your interests to sort out my business.'

'I'd warned you I didn't want the Le Rouzic lad to get me pregnant, but it's been two months now and I still haven't had the decorators in! Do you want a slap?'

It was a strange form of devotion, where the adulterous wife threatened to slap the coloured statue of the sturdy saint. Others proceeded to action. Fragments of plaster broke away and paint chipped off under the leather straps. Oh, the cries coming from Breton heads and chests harder than iron! Their voices howled like the wind. Beneath the lofty vault with its calm swirls of muted light, a superstitious din resounded: a mixture of Catholic faith and heathen practices. The people were transposing on to Saint Yves miracles worked by idols of times past, demanding them with whip strokes, to the great displeasure of a priest who appeared just then.

'Will you stop that! It's madness.'

The rector came running, clutching his liturgical cross and threatening to beat them with it as if it were a club.

'Watch out. My temper is fraying, my stomach's rumbling and my patience is wearing very thin.'

Fat and pink as could be, he hitched up his cassock, and berated his flock. 'Get out of here, you itinerant beggars. Saint Yves doesn't need trouble from you.'

A voice argued, 'That saint is so often absent-minded, lazy or difficult that he doesn't do anything unless he's threatened with violence.'

'Be quiet!' ordered the priest. 'And get rid of that Bas-Breton gullibility. Everything that doesn't belong strictly, exclusively and abundantly to the Roman Catholic Church must be thrown down the pan.'

Someone else protested, 'But, abbé Le Drogo, your little outburst is both laudable and reprehensible at the same time. It's fine for a priest, but coming from a Breton it's bad. In trying to suppress this belief you're diminishing the soul of the Celts. You're throwing our custom to the winds along with the dust of Saint Yves.'

Abbé Le Drogo, with cheeks plump as a pig's bottom, and who lived by Jesus alone, insisted: 'Hitting Saint Yves's statue is just a nonsense! We should breathe nothing but God, in the same way we breathe the fresh air through an open door.'

He lifted high his avenging cross amid the odours of incense. The parishioners scuttled off like deer towards the door of the church.

Back in the dining room at his presbytery, which was done up like a cuckoo clock, the abbé Le Drogo declared, 'Oh, those Bretons who resist the cross and hit Saint Yves – I've given them a reception they won't forget in a hurry. Just let other pilgrims of that sort turn up to whip the saint and I'll be greeting them with a blow in the teeth from a censer.'

'Calm down, dear boy,' advised a mild, elderly man, seated alone at the end of a table almost completely set for the coming lunch. 'Let these people shake off their wretchedness a little. Understand them. They must be really desperate and not know where else to turn before they resort to this idolatry. We may find it stupid, certainly, but when one is completely at a loss, one is ready to clutch at anything, isn't that so?'

'No! We pray to God, and that's it. We leave Saint Yves in peace. Maman's not ready to dine, then?'

'Louise is with your new cook and the two daily women.'

Still muttering – 'After the spring we've had – there's never been deeper poverty caused by inclement weather – the raving minds of the ruined peasants will form a huge midden. That will make for a strange summer for Saint Yves!' – the starving priest pushed open the kitchen door to demand, 'Are we finally going to be able to eat?'

It was the priest's mother, Louise Le Drogo, who turned to her son and replied, 'But, Marcel, *we've* been waiting for *you* while you were at the church.'

'I see the *écuelles* are missing from the table,' the priest yelled at his two daily servants. 'Marguerite André, Françoise Jauffret, do I have to do everything myself – set the table *and* save Saint Yves?'

'Ah, it's still that matter of the statue that has put you in a foul mood,' realised the rector's mother. 'As for our *écuelles*, as you call our plates, rather than bringing in the big serving dish for everyone to put their fingers into, Hélène is suggesting she serves up in the kitchen. In these times of infection, when there's talk of the cholera returning, I do believe it's more hygienic.'

Near the window, Thunderflower pulled the curtain back and watched birds flying in the sky. 'Especially since crows circling over a village mean disease.'

'Fine, fine.'

The grumpy cleric's mood softened at his mother's touch as she accompanied him to the table, caressing his tonsure, saying, 'I know how highly you thought of Anna Jégado, who's gone to

61

the new rector at Bubry to replace the aunt who died so suddenly, but her younger sister, whom you've taken in, seems very good as well. I do believe she's a pearl.'

The pearl being spoken about in the dining room had two of them hooked to her ears – river mussel pearls, which she had had set in cheap steel pendants.

Surrounded by griddles for making pancakes, pots, milk cans, saucepans, skimmers, ladles, a rag ... Thunderflower began to fill pewter plates with a light gruel with honey, each topped with a piece of delicately grilled black pudding. It was then that she noticed another plate, made of blue porcelain, hanging on a wall. The cook grabbed it and placed it in front of her. From behind, Thunderflower could be seen spending a little longer stirring the gruel in that one.

'Right, who'll have this blue plate with the picture of a little Breton girl dancing on the bottom? First I'll give it to Joseph Le Drogo, then to Louise Le Drogo. Next it'll go to ...'

The priest of Guern was at his wits' end.

'Dear Christ, what a shower of shit.'

From a priest's mouth, this was disconcerting.

'What else am I going to have to bear?'

The man, who had been stretching sleepily at daybreak to yawn out his prayers, was now, at the end of the morning, ready to knock down anything that got in his way.

'Saint Yves, how could you allow this to happen?'

Beneath the vault of the church, opposite the statue in its niche, Le Drogo was bathed in tears.

'First of all my father. He fell ill on 20 June and died on the 28th. He was very old, admittedly, but I didn't expect this to happen. He was in fine fettle for his age. Next my mother, who succumbed on 5 July. Yet she wasn't one to go without putting up a fight. I've a good mind to rip your tongue and your eyes out, Saint Yves, and impale you on a spike!'

Inside the Catholic edifice, the parishioners present were stupefied to see their rector tearing strips off the polychrome statue of the Breton saint as he whipped it. 'Bastard! Swine! Here, take that in the face! You've certainly earned it.'

His despair had burst its banks. In the emptiness of the stained-glass windows, heavy with silence, the priest, with his bare fingers, was looking for answers in the reflections.

'But why, Saint Yves? Why?'

The darkness seemed to bark round about him. 'I was so wretched that my sister sent me her seven-year-old daughter to brighten my days a little. And then Marie-Louise Lindevat too, on 17 July? You must be mad, Saint Yves!'

Sorrow rushed into the priest's soul, howling like wind in deserted castles. 'My niece, taken just now as suddenly as if she'd been struck with an axe. Her death was something diabolical. The way that child looked on the infinite ... And somewhere there'll be one more little grave.'

The abbé Le Drogo – Breton through and through – took hold of the saint by the shoulders and shook him violently. 'You knew how much I loved them! When each of these three fell seriously ill, I came in secret to order you to save them. Take this in your stupid face, you idle saint. What good are you, you useless creature?'

Other insults rotted in his mouth. 'What a fate. It's enough to make a man hang himself.'

He swung his liturgical cross against the coloured statue until it came adrift and flew into a thousand pieces on the slabs.

'Saint Yves is dead! He's been unseated. The priest has destroyed him with his stick!'

While the flock ran out of the church shouting to alert the whole village, the abbé Le Drogo went back to the presbytery kitchen where Thunderflower was singing to herself: 'Which day servant shall I give the blue plate to? Ah, Marguerite André.'

'Marguerite André on 23 August, then Françoise Jauffret on 28 September. Both of my day servants.' The priest of Guern was at the table in the dining room at the presbytery, alone. He unfolded his napkin from pure habit as he had lost his appetite (a new phenomenon in this glutton, and he had slimmed down a lot). Thunderflower came into the room carrying the blue plate. Even when the pretty servant walked it was as if she were dancing. She placed the steaming plate in front of her employer.

'It's one of those *soupes aux herbes* I'm so good at making. It will give your heart a good clean out.'

Prematurely aged by his suffering, and holding his head in his hands, the rector wept into his soup. He was worn out by grief and felt profoundly downcast. 'Isn't it beyond comprehension, and simply heartbreaking? What do you think, Hélène?'

'To be honest, what do you expect me to say? Life is short.'

'I'm full to overflowing with horror. What day is it?'

'It's 2 October,' the soubrette by his side informed him.

The abbé Le Drogo dipped a spoon into his soup, and lifted it up, blowing on the steam. He opened his mouth and slipped the spoon in, like the host, amen.

Anna Jégado, in a violet *mantell ganu* (Breton mourning cape) was three years older than her sister, Thunderflower. She had come from Bubry for the funeral and now stood in the kitchen, with the blue plate in her hands. 'It was very kind of you, little sister, to have made that for me before we go to the cemetery. The abbé Le Drogo was very kind as well.'

'Yes, he certainly was, no question about that.'

'Aaargh!' Breaking out in a sudden sweat, Anna began to sway, overcome by dizziness. The kitchen walls were spinning, and the blue plate went flying through the air. Thunderflower rushed to catch it while her older sister collapsed on the floor.

'I'll have to hang it up again. It was almost dropped yesterday.'

The stunningly attractive cook in the presbytery at Guern was holding the blue plate up against the wall, feeling for the nail to hang it on, but she fluffed it and the plate slipped and fell, smashing on the floor. Watched in silence by Dr Martel and the Mayor of Guern, Thunderflower gathered up the remains.

'That said, it would have been of no use to anyone now – I certainly shan't be eating out of it.'

Dr Martel could not get over the shock – not of the plate falling but the carnage.

'What unbelievable cataclysm can have descended on

this house in the space of one summer to wipe out almost all its inhabitants? The wind of death has passed through the presbytery. Perhaps it's the return of the …' The doctor hesitated to say the word aloud.

'Do you think so?' the mayor asked, understanding his meaning.

While Thunderflower untied her apron, Dr Martel recalled: 'Last autumn the cholera claimed more than a hundred lives in Rennes, before the epidemic came to an abrupt end with the frost – it spreads better in the heat. Do these initial deaths, in the summer at the presbytery, herald the curse's passage through Morbihan?'

Into one of the sides of her bag, on the kitchen table, the cook was tidying away two handkerchiefs embroidered with different initials, three napkins, a rosary, a child's doll …

'And if your fears turn out to be justified, Doctor?' the mayor wanted to know.

'Well then, Le Cam, we'll have to get used to it the way we get used to bed bugs or scabies. And if we don't manage to get used to it, then we'll needs die of fear.'

The girl from Plouhinec slipped her arms into the sleeves of a coat and buttoned it up. She was adjusting her collar when the mayor suggested, 'I think it would be wise to refrain from mentioning it for fear of triggering a general panic.'

Marcel shared his opinion. 'It is indeed preferable not to terrify the populace.'

'Right, that's me ready,' said Thunderflower, leather bag over her shoulder. 'May I go?'

'What? Yes, yes …' the mayor said hurriedly.

The cook left the presbytery. She walked under the dim vaults of the church, emerging into daylight through the porch. At the top of the steps she looked at Guern. It was market day with its wealth of honey, butter, leather, tallow and cloth. When people saw her, they called to others, 'Look! It's the one who didn't croak at the priest's house! She's alive.'

A crowd formed around Thunderflower. 'Why didn't *you* snuff it?'

'God saved her. She's a saint,' yelled someone.

The fair lady of Plouhinec was considered an extraordinary being. Her fame was broadcast noisily through the streets. Worried, emotional farmers went down on their knees. It was pitiable! Crowds of other folk came running. Like a flock of scavenging birds, they fell upon the servant, a new figure on whom to focus their attention and curiosity.

Since there was no longer a Saint Yves in the church, she was the one people touched, and of whom they made demands: 'Sainte Yvette, do something to help me!'

'Keep the weevils away from my wheat!'

'I'm having amorous relations with my neighbour but I don't want to find myself pregnant. I'm counting on you, eh; you were saved by a miracle.'

'You've been saved by a miracle, so you can work miracles, can't you?'

Cripples made their way on their crutches, filled with hope. Thunderflower recognised two Norman accents. 'Can't you shtraighten my arm and fix my jaw?' 'Make my eye grow back!' they begged. The wigmakers were in the shafts of their covered cart, pulling it themselves.

From the roof of a house across the road, a tightrope-walking angel of cast iron descended on a cable, carrying a flaming wand. It was a contraption designed to light the pile of straw at the heart of a bonfire hastily got up in honour of Sainte Yvette. Alas, the angel teetered during its journey, and fell on to the wigmakers' cover, which went up in flames. The lettering of 'À la bouclette normande' burnt away while Thunderflower pressed through the crowd, dispensing copious greetings left and right, but complaining: 'The annoying thing now is that I have to find another situation …'

Meanwhile the Normans came rushing past with buckets of water, yelling, 'Sodding Bretons!'

Bubry

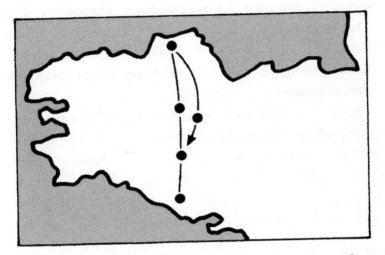

'Then I accept your request for employment ... Hélène. That is your name, isn't it?'

'Yes, Monsieur l'abbé Lorho,' answered Thunderflower, who recognised the door in the kitchen, which still had fixed to it the piece of mirror in front of which her blond hair had first been covered by a headdress.

The young chasubled priest who was speaking to her had a slight stoop. He unfolded his gold spectacles and put them on his nose before turning towards the other, glass door opening on to the courtyard.

'Over there, cutting flowers in front of the presbytery gate, the thin woman you can see with the dry, pockmarked face, that is my sister, Jeanne-Marie Lorho, a very devout maiden lady. She doesn't miss a single Mass. Beside her is my eighteen-year-old niece, Jeanne-Marie Kerfontain, who's also very pious. You'll be our only servant.'

The girl from Plouhinec ran her finger over a very common piece of varnished pottery on the table, fired using poor rushes. 'That wasn't there before, in the abbé Riallan's day.'

'Indeed.'

The priest took off his spectacles and shook hands with Thunderflower to seal the agreement.

'Since there's no one left alive at the presbytery at Guern where you've come from, and your older sister, Anna, who worked here died there too, I'm giving you her place in this clerical household where you will feel at home.'

'Thank you, Monsieur l'abbé Lorho. I'll do my best to serve you well, all three of you if I can manage it.'

Seated demurely in the church at Bubry, Thunderflower was saying the rosary during the early afternoon Mass.

'Maman ... Monsieur Michelet who drove me to my first place ... Godmother ...'

It was the rosary she had brought from Guern. Hélène Jégado's fingers weren't the ones that had worn down the boxwood beads that followed one another: 'Tante Marie-Jeanne, Yann Viltansoù ...'

She gazed at the light of the candles, and listened to the indistinct voice of the gold-spectacled preacher behind the altar. It was the first time she had seen him exercising his ministry. The

70

people he was addressing dissolved into Jesus. The hubbub of their prayers made the church walls sweat, while Thunderflower continued to herself: 'The abbé Le Drogo's father, then his mother ...'

To the right of the porch, a harvester made so bold – during the service too! – as to sharpen his scythe on the edge of the holy water stoup carved out of a menhir, because that would bring good luck for the next crop. The sounds it made mingled with the words of the priest, who was no longer put out by them.

'Tsiing! Tsiing!'

The sound of the blade grating reminded the girl from Plouhinec of the Ankou's scythe.

'Marie-Louise Lindevat ...'

Thunderflower was gazing several rows in front of her, at the back of abbé Lorho's sister, who was kneeling on a prie-dieu, and recognisable from the smallpox scars on the back of her neck. She was wearing a long brown skirt, which had been baked in the oven to fix the folds, and a cap with small turned-up wings. Suddenly, however, the little wings fell down on to her neck and the spinster's back started to move of its own accord, in a fit of shaking.

'Aaargh!'

While the beautiful blonde cook continued her list, with her rosary between her fingers, 'Marguerite André, Françoise Jauffret ...' her employer's sister shot to her feet. She appeared to be feeling a burning inside, so violent that even a dozen cans of milk wouldn't relieve it. She threw herself from side to side, straightened up, bent over again. It was terrible to see. She turned round. Her mouth was gaping, her eyes full of fever.

It was as if all the combined forces of a very dirty trick were producing unbelievable effects on her stomach. She shat herself. Her ankles were drenched in diarrhoea, which ran down into her shoes. It was fortunate that her skirt was brown already, because if not … Tachycardia, dilated pupils, hyperthermia, hallucinations, delirium, agitation, and death caused by paralysis of the respiratory passages.

Beside her, it was her eighteen-year-old niece's turn to stand up. 'Snakes are gnawing at my heart, and tearing my nerves! I'm in boiling oil!'

Jeanne-Marie's nostrils were going like a blacksmith's bellows. Saint Vitus dance set in and she was foaming at the mouth. Meanwhile, Thunderflower was trying not to miss anyone out: 'Abbé Le Drogo, my older sister, Anna …' The priest of Bubry was at a loss at the altar and shouted: 'Euphorbia poultices!' Bluish purple blotches were already appearing on his niece's face. She was seized with terrible vomiting, which erupted in her throat like rolls of thunder.

Clapping her hand over her mouth, she ran down the central aisle towards the porch. But she could not wait and it was in the water stoup that she vomited the remains of kidneys with herbs. Her face was like a drowning woman's as she slumped on to the harvester's scythe.

'No, no! It wasn't me that cut her down,' he protested. 'Look at my blade. There's nothing there. Apart from some bits of kidney, there's not a drop of blood.'

While many in the church clustered frantically round the two dead women, Thunderflower ended with, 'Jeanne-Marie Lorho, Jeanne-Marie Kerfontain,' and stood up.

Crowds can be so fickle. Immediately the pretty cook crossed the porch of the sanctuary, everyone rushed at her with accusations.

'What's happened here is your fault, you've the evil eye! Once before here, when you were thirteen, your godmother …'

'You're a coward.'

'You're the woman who was saved by a miracle yet you bring misfortune with your wickedness!'

'Wickedness in doing what? There's not a scrap of wickedness in me, go on with you,' replied Thunderflower.

The same people who had made her into a saint at Guern (or if not them, then similar ones, idiots at any rate) abhorred Sainte Yvette, now Lily Liver.

'At night you dream of fire, and fire breaks out!'

'You put spells on the animals and blight the corn in the ear.'

'Don't breathe her breath, anyone. It kills!'

Bored and disgusted at the sight of these people – some of whom none the less asked, 'Are you sure about what you're saying?' to which others replied, 'If you can't see the most obvious thing in the world when it's absolutely staring you in the face' – Thunderflower made her way towards the presbytery gate. So what if there were nasty insinuations from countless people to whom she had become a bogeyman? Surrounded by *kornek* headdresses and *capots ribot*, the servant could hear the barking of the spinners and toothless old women trying to grab her by the hair.

'Evil Breton woman.'

'*Ki klanv, ke gant da hent!*' ('Sick bitch, be on your way!')

'When you arrive in a place, death follows. Then when you go away, the evil stops.'

'Ankou! Ankou!'

'Get out of here, you dirty bitch, and don't let us see you in Bubry a third time!'

That same evening, in the priest's mournful drawing room, faced with Lorho's tear-misted gold spectacles, and in the presence of the servant who was busying herself around them, Dr Martel had to admit: 'You can understand the locals' protests, because it's true that there is a link between the deaths at Guern and those at Bubry in the person of Hélène. It may be because there are people who are healthy carriers. It happens that someone carrying the disease transmits it without falling ill themselves. But that's assuredly not the case here, and it's just the result of chance. Cholera morbus is such a strange disease. It begins its ravages then disappears again and no one knows why. It moves to another village, strikes here, spares there, and destroys several members of a family while missing out others and all with no reason. For instance, why are you alive, Father, while your sister and niece …?'

Raising her eyes in exasperation, as she walked between the two men, Thunderflower leapt to the cholera's defence, speaking of it as if it were female. 'Come on now, cholera can't do everything all at once. She's not a machine, you know. You've also got to realise that …'

She carried on towards the kitchen, muttering under her breath, 'For example, I didn't know the priest didn't like kidneys and wouldn't eat them … Otherwise you may be sure I'd have cooked something else for all three of them.'

As she began to peel the vegetables she heard the doctor offer his sincere condolences and leave.

Lorho came to his servant with a handwritten sheet of paper. 'What are you doing, Hélène?'

'Doing? Making your dinner, of course.'

'You mustn't. You have to leave.'

Thunderflower laid the knife on the table. 'You're sending me away, Monsieur l'abbé? So you're just like the rest of the villagers, then.'

'How old are you?'

'Twenty-four.'

'A priest is not permitted to live alone with a female servant under the age of forty. The bishop forbids it. I have to say goodbye to you this evening.'

'This evening? Don't you want me to prepare one last meal for you?'

'Thank you, no.'

Thunderflower had a sense of unfinished business.

'Come now, I'll just whip you up a snack before I go, and you can eat it on your own presently.'

'Don't insist, Hélène.'

'I had in mind something you really love, *poulouds* – those flour balls cooked with …'

'No, please don't.'

'A bowl of milk then, at least – boiled with some chervil for its aniseed flavour. I'll bring it to you in the drawing room right away.'

'No, really. So that you easily find another situation, I've written this letter of recommendation praising you most highly.

In it you're described as particularly clean and an excellent cook.'

'Could you add that I'm renowned for my *soupe aux herbes*, and then put that I've invented a very good cake as well? As for the kidneys with herbs, let's not make a thing of it, they're not to everyone's taste.'

Locminé

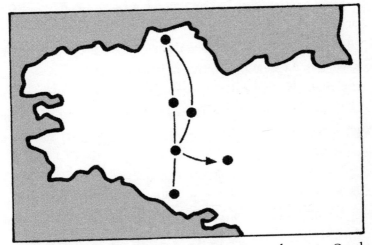

Thunderflower hurried from one bedroom to the next. On the poorly lit staircase of the narrow house, she muttered, 'I'm sure I'm going to fall and kill myself.' She went from the one sick woman in bed on the first floor to the other on the second. 'First Jeanne-Marie Leboucher, now for her daughter, Perrine.'

On sturdy, untiring legs she climbed back up the stairs. Both the mother and her twenty-year-old child were critically ill. How sad!

'It's such a pity to go to so much trouble for nothing,' lamented Thunderflower, 'since they're both going to die.'

'How can you know that?' asked the doctor, bag in hand, on the first-floor landing. He was wearing a wide-skirted coat and a beaver-skin hat.

'Well, Dr Toursaint, all your remedies *do* have the opposite effect from the one you expect,' the servant replied helpfully. 'With both the dying women, the cures are behaving counter to their known properties.'

'That's true, but …' Toursaint said defensively. 'I'm only a doctor in a Bas-Breton village, not a bigwig in Rennes! What's that white powder you're mixing in that glass, Hélène?'

'It's from the bottle you told me to get from the pharmacy.'

'Oh, yes, the quinine sulphate to treat fevers.'

In the leather gaiters that went out by night, even in winter and along the worst roads, trying to bring help with the little knowledge he had, Dr Toursaint went into the first-floor bedroom.

'How are you feeling, Madame Leboucher?'

'Since even the water from Melusine's spring, which you prescribed, hasn't cured me – I've drunk from it three times at midnight – I'm giving up remedies.'

'Now now, Jeanne-Marie, what's all this? I think you simply have an attack of acrodynia, an illness that is causing the intense pins and needles in your limbs and the violent burning in your stomach. But, I say, what about your cook, her devotion and how involved she is in what happens to you?'

'Thank goodness Hélène's here. I don't know what would have become of us without her. For more than sixty hours now she's been looking after Perrine and me, without eating any of the food she's brought us, and with no sleep. She lavishes us with continual attentions.'

Speaking of attentions, Hélène was just then administering them to the Leboucher daughter in bed on the floor above.

'Look, here's a glass of stuff you have to drink on the orders of the doctor I passed on the stairs. I think he called it quinine sulphate.'

Perrine struggled to swallow even a mouthful but none the less ordered, 'Give me the rest to drink.'

'Yes, certainly.'

No sooner had the brew been consumed than a sudden pallor came over her and her lips shrank back. There was an abrupt increase in the size of her pupils, and her eyes grew wider. Her eyelids began to twitch wildly. Seated at the bedside, Thunderflower could see her own outline in the foamy bubbles appearing at the edge of the invalid's mouth. Then she walked back and forth in front of the window, the daylight casting her pretty shadow on to the bedroom floor at each turn, and all the while she told the patient a legend: a knight returning from a journey came upon a woman shivering with fever at the roadside. He lifted her up on to his horse and carried her into the town. It was the plague. Thunderflower came over to Perrine again and, leaning in close to her, predicted the future: 'You're going to die, my girl.'

In the room below, Dr Toursaint was absentmindedly reading the letter of recommendation the servant had brought, which was on the mantelshelf. There he read: 'Hélène Jégado is an excellent cook and my one regret is that I cannot keep her until I die.' Just then he heard a cry, piercing as a horn, through the ceiling. He rushed for the stairs and pushed open the door of the second bedroom to find Perrine dead in her bed, with the cover pulled up over her face.

'I'm more doubtful about medicine than I've ever been,' he moaned, while Thunderflower went downstairs to the mother.

On the staircase she half opened her lips, revealing small, bright white teeth, like those of a proverbial she-wolf.

'What was that cry that sent the doctor running, Hélène?' asked Jeanne-Marie Leboucher, struggling to sit up in bed.

'It was your daughter who ...'

'Who?'

'Who.'

For the mother in her current state, the shock was too great. There was nothing to stop her sinking into the abyss. Her maternal love stumbled through the burning of this hell and as her head fell back onto the pillow she grew radiant.

'Well then, let's sleep the last sleep. God will take care of our awakening ...'

'That's it,' said Thunderflower, encouragingly. 'That's what you have to say.'

Next there was a long rattling noise in Jeanne-Marie Leboucher's chest, before she turned her face to the wall and became motionless by the time the doctor arrived – too late.

'The lettuce water she was given, and the gomme syrup won't have helped at all, then. Perhaps it was typhoid fever.'

The cook got hold of a pitcher, blew out the candles and covered a bowl with a cloth, to Pierre-Charles Toursaint's astonishment.

'What are you doing, Hélène?'

'When someone has breathed their last, you have to put out the candles while the soul passes, and also be careful that it doesn't turn the milk or drown in the jug of water. Right, that's done. I'm worn out. What I really need now is to go out for a pick-me-up.'

Outside, under her lace-trimmed headdress, Thunderflower was walking behind a cart that had lost its cover, and whose charred and twisted metal hoops had suffered a fire. In front of the vehicle, each pulling one shaft, two Normans were complaining about the state of the Breton road, their accent ringing out: 'All the Locminé roadsh need to be redone.'

'You can't take one step after dark without risking a broken leg.'

The cook looked at the rectangular bales wrapped in rough canvas, which lined the wagon she was following. Through the triangular tears at the corners of the pink fabric packages burst very unerotic-looking big black tufts of long, stinking Breton hair. Shaken about by the uneven road surface, in the light of a tavern from which laughter and singing could be heard they looked like rustic pubic hair dancing a *fest-noz*.

The wigmakers continued along the narrow road, where the littler one's shadow made a misshapen gnome on a wall, as, apropos of the lost cover, he had to concede, 'Well, it'sh not raining, that'sh shomething.'

'It keeps the hair in better condition,' the bald man agreed.

Thunderflower went into the bar. From the dim street, through the lighted windows made up of little squares of coloured glass, a beautiful girl was visible – green eyes, blond curls escaping from her headdress, skin with a scent of vanilla and sex, and which must taste of it as well. The landlady came towards her. 'What do you want, Hélène?'

'Some of your brandy, Widow Lorcy.'

*

Locminé was a picturesque village, with its elm trees, its openwork steeple, its narrow grey houses, and its graveyard, which Thunderflower had just left to return to the late Widow Lorcy's bar, where a grieving niece was waiting for her.

'My aunt died the very next morning after the evening she took you on here. Why?'

'How should I know? That's been the case so often. Death follows me everywhere I go. When I went to the presbytery at Guern there were seven people there. When I departed, I was the one closing the door behind me. At Bubry I saw the priest's sister and niece die. I arrived in Locminé, at Jeanne-Marie Leboucher's, and she died, and Perrine as well. And now your poor aunt. You couldn't exactly say I bring good luck. Would you like a piece of the cake I made? The widow Lorcy barely started it.'

'No thank you, I'm not hungry,' the niece answered.

'All right, too bad. Someone else can have it.'

The not over-talented Dr Pierre-Charles Toursaint arrived in great distress at the bar, where millers slaked their thirst – an establishment the niece, who had inherited, had no intention of keeping on.

'I don't know what your aunt died of either,' he said. 'Something wrong with the pylorus, perhaps. At any rate, applying leeches and vesicatories proved useless. I also tried to get the fever to go into the bark of a tree, but in vain. The only good fortune she had was the constant and zealous care Hélène lavished on her, just as she did at the Lebouchers'. You poor servant,' he added, turning to Thunderflower, 'you must be very tired.'

'I'm all right. A little tired but, after all, I haven't come to Locminé to enjoy myself.'

'And you're without an employer yet again?'

'Well, yes, they're rotting in the graveyard.'

'Hélène, my parents are looking for a cook. Their previous one didn't suit. When she talked about her soup, my mother used to say, "If only it was dishwater we could have fed the pigs on it."'

'She wouldn't complain about my *soupe aux herbes*,' Thunderflower said firmly.

'My father, mother and sister live in a town house along with their housemaid. Would you be prepared to join the four of them this very day, 9 May?'

The girl from Plouhinec turned her head towards the coloured glass in a window so that the doctor could not see her expression, which was like a weasel's when it spies a dovecote.

On 12 May, Pierre-Charles Toursaint was crunching along the gravel path in his leather gaiters. On the doctor's right was his sister, on his left his parents. All four were making their way towards a poor peasant couple to whom they condescendingly offered the standard expressions of sympathy.

'Our sincere condolences, Madame and Monsieur Eveno. We shall miss your daughter, Anna. She was a most pleasant housemaid who, alas, died so suddenly under our roof.' The grieving parents answered each member of the family in Breton: '*Trugaré*.' ('Thank you.') They said the same to the new cook, who had likewise come to offer the fraternal sympathy she rarely had opportunity to use. The housemaid's body, wrapped in a sewn-up white sheet, slid along a plank and plummeted into the common grave. As soon as the first spadefuls of earth had been thrown on to the sheet, Thunderflower took her leave: 'Right, I'm off to do the cooking!'

15 May. 'He is neither cold nor hot, he is not dead, he's sleeping. The dawn comes in vain, he sleeps.' An open fan in front of Thunderflower's face did not hide her burst of laughter. Over the top of the fan, her lovely eyes were watching a dignitary speaking in the same cemetery, where the eye was now drawn to a dozen wreaths around a hole. 'To our father', 'To my husband'. Dr Toursaint and his sister were holding up their fainting mother, who was wearing a blue widow's cape. Some women in headdresses with fluttering or turned-up edges, and dressed in black, were there like carrion crows, watching what was happening around them. As the crowd began to disperse, Thunderflower announced, folding up her fan, 'Ah me, that's another one then. And to think it won't be the last …' The prediction resounded in the ears of the Breton women walking in the tranquil cemetery where little white crosses bloomed in the shade of the gothic church.

On 18 May, the sky was overcast and the ground damp. Thunderflower found the people who had come for the burial ugly. Dr Toursaint had his arms round his mother, who could no longer stand unaided: 'My daughter as well …' She answered her neighbours' greetings with '*Trugaré*' and the vague gesture of an old lady who is crying. As reddish light washed over the trees, anger darkened the brows of the Bretons approaching that perfect beauty, the cook. 'How many deaths is that now since you've been in our village? Even just at the Toursaints', how many?' Hélène brushed off the question, saying, 'Let Death count the dead!' There was a grinding of teeth: 'The cemetery won't be big enough if that girl stays in Locminé.' Among themselves they likened her to the innards of a hanged bitch. 'Destruction is in you. You're possessed. You bring misfortune,' they told her.

While the sly Morbihan women went into the hydrangeas and began removing the needles and pins from their headdresses and bodices, Thunderflower, knowing what they had in mind, prudently beat a hasty retreat from the cemetery. In silence, taking the road where grass was growing up between the stones, she returned to her masters' house (well ... just her elderly mistress's from now on) where a wisp of smoke could be seen rising from the chimney above the kitchen. Oh, the meat that was cooking, and the cake that followed!

20 May. 'It is with great sorrow that Dr Toursaint announces the death of his mother ...' Stuck to the outside wall of the town hall at Locminé, the death notice fluttered in the wind while on the façade of the Toursaint house, written in charcoal by an anonymous hand, were the words, 'People are murdered here.' In the drawing room of his parents' house, the village doctor was utterly bewildered.

'I've lost my whole family. Their house has completely emptied in little more than a week ...'

He was lamenting to the President of the society of good

works, who had come to offer support in his cruel trial. She said in surprise, 'Pierre-Charles, I don't see your cook, who was also absent from the burial, I think.'

'Yes, Hélène vanished at first light without even asking for her wages, but you can see her point of view. Given all the superstitions being heaped on her, and people's fear of her, that beautiful woman chose to keep out of sight. If she'd come to the cemetery for this latest burial, just imagine what the villagers would have done to her. In Basse-Bretagne there's such a strong belief that evil characters from legend really exist.'

Squeak … squeak … As she walked along the road leading to Auray, with her bag over one shoulder, the road stretching ahead of her, but her thoughts elsewhere, Thunderflower suddenly heard a sound like a squeaking axle behind her.

Squeak, squeak.

'That's not the noise of a carriage drawing nearer and about to overtake me. I'd have heard it in the distance.'

Squeak, squeak.

The shrill creaking was growing ever louder, ever closer. It was deafening, echoing even close up.

Squeak, squeak!

'Is it the Ankou's cart?'

The girl from Plouhinec turned round. There was nothing behind her. The servant continued on her way.

'Oh, it's me then.'

Auray

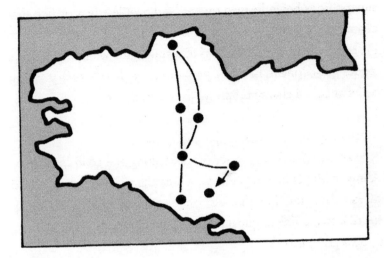

Squeak, squeak!

'What's wrong with you, Hélène, that you keep making that noise like a squeaking axle with your teeth while clutching your forehead? Headache?'

'It's because, Mother Superior, I so much want to cook for all the Sisters of Charity of Saint-Louis at the Convent of the Eternal Father.'

'Oh, no, don't start that again, Hélène. For more than a year now I've been telling you, we already have a cook.'

'Sister Athanase, let me take her place just for one meal. It's really important to me.'

The Mother Superior, a tall commanding presence in the

middle of the convent common room, stretched wide the sleeves of her severe dark brown habit and raised her voice to Thunderflower, who sat hunched up on a spartan bench.

'Hélène, when you came to offer your services at the Eternal Father, just as we were looking for a maid, you accepted this job inside the convent because you wished to flee the outside world for a time, I don't know why.'

'Alas, I had an unfair reputation for making too much work for pharmacists by destroying human bodies … Well, I shall just have to nourish you in my own way. Without my recipes I'm fading away, withering like a flower deprived of water.'

'I'm not going to give in to your whim, Hélène.'

'You call it a whim when what I'm talking about is a mission.'

'Oh, yes, the great mission of boiling three boxes of carrots and putting a dozen rabbits on a spit for a convent,' guffawed the Mother Superior, her chest bouncing and, with it, the wooden cross hanging from a string around her neck.

'I'd make baby Jesuses out of sugar for you to swallow as communion wafers.'

'Don't argue, Hélène. Get your broom and pail and go and clean the sisters' rooms. You will also cut a new altar cloth from the fabric that abbé Olliveau brought yesterday. And don't forget to dust the musical instrument in the common room. That's something you too often forget. Quick now!'

The servant went off, trailing her broom. From a window she noticed pine trees communing with the stars. It also seemed as if the wind were whispering messages.

*

'Sister Athanase, Sister Athanase! Look at my nun's habit!'

'What *are* you doing, Sister Sophie, with your breasts bare for all to see?'

'I found my robe like this when I woke up, with two holes cut out of the chest.'

'Sister Athanase, Sister Athanase! Look at me with my back to you.'

'Have you taken leave of your senses, Sister Marie-Thérèse, coming to show me your bare backside in the common room? Turn round to face me! No, don't turn round. Behind you, Christ hanging on the wall above the harmonium might see your buttocks.'

'Someone's cut a big round piece out of the lower back.'

'Sister Athanase, a triangle's been taken out of the front of my habit, right in the middle.'

'And here's Sister Augustine come to show me her bush and we've not even had breakfast yet. Will you turn round, Sister Marie-Thé— No, not you! Sister Augustine. Oh, my goodness gracious!'

Once she had seen, among other things, a nun's habit cut very short like a chemise and asserted, 'You've got good legs, Sister Agnes,' and heard Sister Madeleine claiming, 'Don't you think I look like an African savage with my habit all cut into strips?' the Mother Superior could take no more of the crazy fashion parade, and exploded, 'Go and get changed, all of you.'

'We can't, Sister Athanase. Not one outfit's been spared.'

'It's because you don't take proper care of your things!' yelled the Mother Superior, holding her arms up to heaven, while Sister Denise, bare armed, warned her, 'The bottom of your habit's been crenellated. You look like a fortress tower that's been turned upside down.'

'Oh, which of you has carried out this vestimentary attack in the convent?' thundered the woman in charge of the Sisters of Charity of Saint-Louis.

'Perhaps it wasn't a sister,' murmured a nun.

'Then, who?'

'The maid's been acting rather strangely in recent days.'

All the nuns, each with missal in hand, crowded around the Mother Superior, almost stifling her as they gossiped in low voices. 'How many times have we come upon her speaking to someone invisible, stretching out her arms to them?' said one, whose buttocks were exposed. Another, bare breasted, backed her up. 'It's true that there's some imaginary being she gives a very strange name to and whose presence she seems to be checking on.' The one with the al fresco bush recalled, 'Yesterday I heard her telling it she wanted to model herself on it at all costs.' Another, all in strips of cloth, explained, 'It seems she's the only one who can hear this great mysterious voice and her mission is to act as a channel for it.' The Sisters of Charity of Saint-Louis, who spoke to God personally on a daily basis, were shocked rigid by the servant's madness.

A great silence reigned in the common room when suddenly a nun who went to say a prayer aloud let out a cry: 'Look, my missal! Oh! On every page with engravings, the faces of Christ and of the Virgin have been torn out.'

'Mine too!'

'And mine!'

'Same here.'

All the nuns were aghast at the books in which the heads of their Christian idols had been cut off.

'It's witchcraft.'

'Be quiet! Don't say that word, not ever!' interrupted the Mother Superior in her dress with battlements – a fortress impregnable by devilish superstitions. 'I don't want to hear another word about this. Each of you, take a bowl of milk and go and have breakfast modestly in your rooms while I think things over in my study.'

Cleared of exhibitionist nuns, the common room at last fell silent again. Through the door at the far end, Thunderflower entered with her broom and a full pail. She paused beneath the Christ hanging on the wall when through another, half-open door a yell was heard. Sister Athanase came running at top speed, the jagged edge of her habit flapping at her ankles, and moaned, 'What next? There's been nothing but uproar here since dawn. Lucky it's a place for contemplation, isn't it?'

'She ... she ... she,' stammered a nun, pointing at the maid at the end of the room. 'She's em ... em ... emptied in the instru—'

'What then? Out with it!'

'She's emptied the slops pail into the harmonium.'

Behind the musical instrument whose lid was still up, Thunderflower put the iron container down on the tiles, and did not deny it.

The Mother Superior was one of those people who continually get upset over a trifle but stay terribly calm when the situation is very serious. She walked towards the servant. 'You dare to empty a slops pail into the harmonium of the Eternal Father? Who or what are you? You're certainly not human.'

'Humans hold no sway over me, none at all,' replied the accused, brazenly. 'No humiliation will lay me low, no reef will sink me, and no hammer flatten me. I cannot be destroyed.'

'Get out of this convent, Hélène. News of you will spread round all the religious places of Morbihan and you'll never find another situation. However, I shall say nothing in town about the extraordinary events that have occurred here, because you're quite capable of denying all involvement and then the peasants would sit round the fire of an evening, saying that it was korrigans, fairies, sirens, or hairy Poulpiquets who did it – or goodness knows what other legendary creature of this Celtic land.'

The closing words of this speech did not exactly please Thunderflower, who had been nourished on precisely this enchanted but terrifying milk of evening storytelling, and on the energy of the menhirs against which she had leant as a child to feel the soul of the standing stones. Something like a rumble of pebbles rose, swirling up in the water, from deep in her throat. 'Our legends, or even the comic routines of fairground Harlequins, make perfect sense compared to the sermons, and jokes of priests and Mother Superiors ...'

'Get out!'

'What, that creature's still in Auray? And, what's worse, she's with your parents-in-law, Dr Doré?'

In a dining room belonging to a bourgeois family with private means, which contained a bird cage alive with the sounds of canaries and greenfinches, the table was splendidly set for dinner.

'Which creature, abbé Olliveau? Who are you speaking about?'

Around twenty guests, glass in hand, exchanged toasts and walked around before they went into ecstasies over the dishes laid out on the long white tablecloth – trout, lovely eels, mallards, and side dishes in sauces of various colours.

'Dr Doré, I'm talking about the girl I saw at the ovens when I passed the open door of the kitchen.'

'Hélène?'

'That's it. What's her surname?'

'How should I know? No one asks a servant their last name. The first one's enough. I believe she told me only that she was from Kerhordevin in Plouhinec.'

The subtle odours of the game and the freshwater fish tickled the nostrils of gourmet dignitaries anxious to take their places at table, while the abbé Olliveau took the doctor's arm and led him to the end of the room.

'Doctor, like every priest in Morbihan I've made an oath to the Mother Superior of the Eternal Father, and so I'm not going to tell you what your Hélène did at the convent, but if you knew … I'll say only that for years now, in every presbytery and village where that girl has been a cook, people have died in unexplained ways. She uses witchcraft to cut down humans.'

'Witchcraft? Father, surely it's a distressing anachronism for such an odious expression to come from the mouth of a cleric?'

'There are so many bad rumours about her.'

'Pah, they're just made up. She gave us excellent references – from a priest, as it happens. And we have nothing but praise for her work. I've even asked her if she knows another cook of the same calibre for the Mayor of Pontivy, who despairs of ever finding one to suit.'

'She has an infirmity, a sort of horrible goitre. People even claim she's the Ankou.'

'Monsieur le curé, you're sunk in the prejudices of a bygone age.'

A lady wearing the violet stockings of a married woman walked past the fire crackling in the grate. Apparently the mistress of the house, she had dotted her headdress with as many little mirrors as she had hundreds of livres of income. Reflecting the candle flames, the tiny looking-glasses shot rays of light all over the dining room. She shone like a lighthouse. In black velvet, a sign of wealth (she had a lot of velvet in her dress), and with her shoulders covered in a shawl with a brightly coloured foliage pattern, this ever so proper lady sat down at the head of the table and summoned Dr Doré.

'Come and eat, Son-in-law. Just seeing the marvels Hélène has prepared for us is making my mouth water. When we envisaged this meal, which is so important for your ambition to be mayor, she promised us a banquet that would go down in the annals of Auray. I see now that was no lie. Now, let's be seated.'

'We're coming, Mother-in-law.'

But in his panic, the priest held him back with both hands, insisting, 'Send your cook away right now! So many tombs have been opened and closed on her path already, and more will open this evening if you don't act.'

'The meal's ready.'

'Have it thrown away.'

'You can't mean that. The support of my guests is indispensable if I want to become the chief magistrate of Auray. How can I go and tell them, "Actually, I've changed my mind. You can all go home hungry"?'

'I'm telling you, all hell's going to be let loose by this girl. And tomorrow I'll be saying the Office of the Dead for you all.'

The son-in-law raised his eyebrows at the prediction.

'But are you sure it's her, this monster of yours? You don't even know her surname, and Hélène's—'

'I saw her when I took fabric to the Eternal Father for their altar cloth,' the priest said emphatically. 'Prevent the massacre while there's still time, and send the cook packing.'

Dr Doré looked at his guests, already seated at table. They were unfolding their napkins in front of a pretty porcelain dish filled with a delicate green soup, which had been cooling for a moment or two. They were tapping on their spoons, to hasten the arrival of the priest and future mayor so they could start. At the head of the table, his mother-in-law could wait no longer. 'Right, I'm going to begin, otherwise it'll be cold.'

She raised her spoon to her mouth and was repeating the gesture when her son-in-law cried out, 'No! Don't eat it, Mother-in-law!'

'And why not? This *soupe aux herbes* is delicious.'

They were all gathered round the mother-in-law in bed in her room. She was foaming at the mouth, and jerking about as if being electrocuted.

'What's the matter with her?'

She gave a hiccup and died.

'Where's Hélène?' the priest asked her son-in-law.

'Well now, I don't know. You told me to send her away. I did so on the spot, as I handed her her bag.'

'We've got to find her!'

'Oh, make up your mind, abbé Olliveau.'

Pontivy

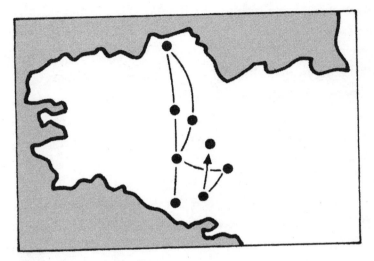

'Goodness, it's raining!'

'Oh yesh, I felt a shpot too.'

The two Norman wigmakers rested the ends of their cart shafts on the stones and looked up at the clouds from which a sudden downpour was falling.

'It's pouring! Let's hope it doesn't damage the bales of hair,' fretted the bald man.

'It'sh only a shquall,' said the short, crooked one with the dislocated jaw, hopefully.

'Only a squall?' said the tall one-eyed man, doubtfully, continuing to examine the overcast sky.

'It'sh 3 March, so it'sh an April shower.'

'While we're in Rue du Fil, with all the trades related to cloth, we should buy some to make a new cover to stretch over the charred hoops of the cart.'

'With what? If we shpend the little money we shtill have, how will we pay for the next lot of hair? Don't worry. The rain will go over.'

'Go over, go over.'

Under the awning of a nearby bar, Thunderflower was sheltering from the torrential rain, which threatened to ruin the ribbons of her headdress. She was paying no attention to the two Normans, who slid under their vehicle, promising each other between its wheels, 'I'm not pulling the cart any further while it's raining like this.'

'Neither am I.'

The cook was looking across the road to where an ivy-covered house stood surrounded by a wall. Thunderflower rushed through the puddles to reach the covered entrance gate. Mesmerised by a statue mounted in the wall beside it, she pulled the bell chain then, impatient, pulled it again as it was raining so hard. Soon she heard a door slam, the sound of footsteps hurrying across gravel and a key turning in the lock of the gate, which opened.

'Who's that?' demanded Thunderflower immediately, pointing to the statue.

'Saint Thuriau,' a man's voice replied. Its owner was holding a streaming wet coat over his head for protection. 'We owe him numerous miracles, including the resurrection of a young girl.'

'What's resurrection?'

'Bringing a dead person back to life.'

'You wouldn't catch me doing that,' smiled Thunderflower, stepping into the courtyard.

'And who are you?' asked the man who had opened the gate, as they climbed the steps to the house.

The woman from Plouhinec replied in Breton, 'They call me Hélène. Otherwise, who I am you'll find out soon … to your cost.'

Hanging his soaking wet coat on a hook in the kitchen, on whose glass roof the millions of torrential drops were beating, the gentleman instructed her, 'Speak to me in French, Madame.'

'I was saying, Monsieur Jouanno, that the future Mayor of Auray thinks that I'm a cook who might suit you as the current Mayor of Pontivy.'

'That's very thoughtful of the good Dr Doré. How is he?'

'He's well. His mother-in-law, on the other hand, could really do with Saint Thuriau.'

'Really?'

There was a noise of galloping on the staircase, mixed with animal shrieks and the cries, shrill and very deep by turns, of an adolescent boy whose voice was breaking.

'I've got one, Papa! I caught another one in the gutter.'

The other door of the glass kitchen, the one leading into the house, was suddenly flung wide to reveal an overexcited acne-ridden youth gripping a struggling cat in his outstretched fists. The feline bared its teeth and spat. Its paws were rigid, claws out. Trapped by the neck and lower back, despite desperate squirming it found itself plunged into a sink filled with boiling washing-up water. Greasy, iridescent spatters flew in all directions, hitting the panes of the glasshouse. They ran down the windows in parallel to the squally rain on the other side of the glass. When the drowned cat had stopped moving, the youth flung it on the floor like a steaming washcloth, before grabbing a saucepan.

'I'm off to tie this to a dog's tail in the street. It'll send it mad. Give me one of your ribbons so I can tie a knot.'

He ripped a piece from the servant's soaking, loose headdress. A stoic Thunderflower smiled as her eyes fell on a fly-paper, while the father interposed, 'Émile, you might at least say good day to our new cook.'

'I don't talk to maids,' retorted Émile Jouanno, slamming the door on to the gravel courtyard behind him.

'Émile, it's raining!' his father called after him. 'Take your coat, you'll make yourself ill.'

'I don't care a jot.'

His father gave a sigh. 'Ah, children. Especially when one's looking after them on one's own. Do you have any yourself?'

'No. If I fell pregnant one day, I'd get rid of it.'

'Despite being a good administrator and a mayor justly respected by his fellow citizens, I can't control my only son, for whom every nasty trick is a badge of honour. He's very rowdy, beating up his schoolmates and burning his stomach violently by refusing to eat anything but mustard or drink anything but vinegar. You'll have to keep those substances hidden at all times, as they're so harmful to his health. That's the only instruction I will not compromise on.'

'So your son's partial to things that set fire to the innards, then?'

'I'd like you to make him lovely sweet things, creams and milky dishes, which he'll get a taste for if they're delicious. Maybe that will calm him down.'

*

Some days later in the glass kitchen, Thunderflower was wiping the steam from a pane with her finger so she could watch the gusts of wind and rain ruining the mimosas in the courtyard, when Émile Jouanno, aged fourteen, came in, yelling, 'I'm famished. Where's the mustard? Get me some to eat, you bitch!'

The cook, who was now scraping the bottom of a saucepan, turned round, spoon in hand, and very offended: 'What a badly brought-up child! Never in any household, my man, has anyone shown me such a lack of respect! On your father's instructions, I'm making you a delicate vanilla compote.'

'Then you know where you can stick it.'

Émile Jouanno was making a mistake in speaking to Thunderflower like that while she was cooking him something to eat, but youth is often imprudent. After the servant had eyed the steam from her compote and murmured in Breton, 'You strange little creature. I aim to do you harm; allow me a hope of succeeding,' the uncouth boy reminded her, 'You've already been told we speak only French here, you bumpkin from standing-stone land. Where's the vinegar? I'm thirsty.'

'So is death,' declared Hélène Jégado, wheeling round abruptly on her heels. 'Drink this milk I've prepared for you. You'll see, it prickles too.'

As soon as the glass was empty, the cook instructed the boy, 'Now go and lie down, my lad, since you've got stomach ache.'

'No I haven't. Even vinegar doesn't ... Aaaaargh! Help!'

'See, what did I tell you? But you never listen.'

The spotty youth collapsed in a heap on the floor. Beside a

dresser with plates on its shelves, the servant knelt down by the still conscious Émile and confessed, 'I'm the Ankou who travels through Brittany. I have stuck my scythe in your heart and will turn your blood as cold as iron.'

She wiped the sweat from the boy's forehead with her hand, adding, 'It's not because you're wicked that I'm doing this. Even if you were kind it would be just the same. This way, to be honest, it's a pleasure, though. You're someone I shan't miss. Be assured of my utter contempt.'

Shaking her victim a little to make sure he was dead, the cook took a deep dish for the compote and got to her feet. As she straightened up she noticed her shadow, still slender-waisted, growing longer on the wall of the house. She removed her headdress and unpinned her chignon, letting her hair fall over her shoulders. Its outline now resembled the Ankou's hood. Next the woman from Plouhinec put her right arm straight up in the air, holding the dish by its edge. The shadow of her raised limb looked like the long handle of an agricultural tool and, as Thunderflower tilted it this way or that, the dish described the curved blade of a scythe.

The door on to the courtyard opened, allowing in a burst of rain and the father, who asked the servant, 'What are you doing holding that plate in the air?'

'Daydreaming ...'

'Poor Hélène, you'd do better to— Oh, Émile! What's happened to him?'

*

The next morning, the Mayor of Pontivy was standing in the kitchen, wearing the blue outfit of full mourning. He unfolded a letter near his servant, who was sitting on a chair, lethargically calm. The din of the rain splashing against the panes of the glass room could be heard, and then the father's voice as he read the words on the sheet of paper aloud.

'8 March 1838. Autopsy report. Émile Jouanno. Inflammation of the stomach. Corrosion of the intestines, which may be attributed to recent inordinate consumption of mustard and vinegar.'

The hand holding the letter dropped back along the thigh of the town's chief magistrate, who spoke bitterly: 'I'd told you, "Dangerous substances have to be kept hidden."'

'That's what I do, Monsieur.'

'My son's death proves otherwise.'

'But—'

'Hélène, you will have to look for a new situation.'

Thunderflower stood up, put on her coat, threw her bag over her shoulder and set out again. As she closed the gate behind her, she hailed the statue of Saint Thuriau, 'Give my regards to Madame the Virgin, not forgetting the Trinity.'

Suddenly the heavy rain clouds hanging in the sky above Rue du Fil burst into hail. The little balls of ice rattled on the roofs, ricocheting off the sheet metal. Very rapidly tons of them fell on the ground. The Rue du Fil, turned to silver, gleamed. The two Normans walked round their cart in utter disbelief: 'It can't be true. That's not po-po-possible.' They skidded on the words just as their shoes, worn down by years of pulling the cart, went sliding on the loose hailstones. They fell over, got up again. They were like two shipwreck survivors from the sky. They held on to each other, arm in arm, as if about to do a Breton circle dance. Fragments of wood flew off the wobbly trellises of their vehicle's sides, and the ruined cloth of the bales on the floor of the cart split open in any number of places. The tall one-eyed man, who would have torn his hair out, had he had any left, grabbed tufts of the hair escaping through the holes pierced by the celestial machine gun. He could have cried. 'Our goods are going to be ruined.'

Everything was losing its shape and being spoilt. And what a racket the storm of ice marbles made! When one of the men shouted, 'Lie on top of the bales, that'll protect them,' the other replied, 'I can't hear you.' They laughed so much they fell over again.

For the cook who was leaving, the hail was like an onslaught of pins and needles thrown from a catapult, in order to drive her from the town. She felt herself the target of the succeeding gusts, but did not care a fig. Alone amid the shameful wreckage of her private catastrophe, Thunderflower walked on, arms outstretched before her. Her palms, turned upwards to the sky, and soon filled with pools of light, occasionally took flight like white birds, while behind her the wigmakers, submerged in an enormous nightmare, were struggling like swimmers, yelling, 'What foul weather! You'd think we were fish, there's so much water around us. We'll be growing scales at this rate. Why did we ever come to this shit-hole of a Brittany?'

Hennebont

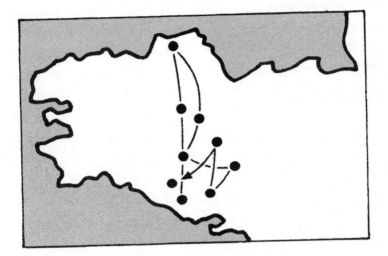

In a dim bedroom, which was also a study, the curtains were still closed and an old man so decrepit he was deformed was taking his time over getting up. To make the journey from his marquetry box-bed to an ancient armchair with carvings of people on it, fashioned in Solomon's time no doubt, he first clutched on to a Cornish clock, then puffed his way along the stone mantel of the fireplace where a dying fire still glimmered. Standing in the doorway of his kitchen, Thunderflower – radiantly beautiful – was teasing him.

'Monsieur Kerallic, if you go at that speed, you'll be old by the time you reach your chair!'

'But I am old, Hélène. I'm weary, no longer of an age for hiking. Like a chess piece, I move rarely.'

Wearing an ultramarine-blue dressing gown, he made his way past the stuffed animals, and insects preserved in spirits of wine, saying sadly, 'The years have left snow on my temples but, when all's said and done, having lived without much joy I shall die without great regret. How is it that you came to me at dawn, shaking me by the shoulder as I lay in bed and whispering in my ear, "The time has come, you stubborn old man. We'll have to get going. My name is Hélène"? Had I left the door unlocked as if I were hoping you'd come?'

'I was on my way to Lorient when, as I walked up one of the steep streets of Hennebont, a voice told me what to do: "Pay a visit to Kerallic, the old schoolteacher, first. He's tired of living and will have a job for you." So I said to myself, "Right, I'll just look in and make his early morning coffee because I'll have to prepare the midday meal somewhere else."'

'Will you be leaving again so soon?'

'I've a lot of people to visit, Monsieur Kerallic. If I tarry with all of them I'll never get through my quota.'

'What are you talking about?'

'I'll go and see to the coffee,' answered the servant girl, turning back towards the kitchen.

The elderly man flopped into his chair between a volume of Celtic tales on one arm and a Hebrew grammar on the other, beside his table cluttered with papers, books and newspapers. His smoky lamp, lit by the visitor, cast a feeble light on him as he went on talking about how tired and weary he was: 'It seems that what is wrong with me is a sort of fog in my head, which makes it hard for me to distinguish between dreams and reality.'

Hélène's voice sounded from the kitchen: 'I've got that too, Monsieur Kerallic.'

'Really, Hélène – at your age?'

'Sometimes I don't know any more …'

Coming back into the room with a wooden box-like object in her hand, she asked, 'Is this for grinding coffee?'

'Yes, it's new. A present from a former pupil of mine who is now the doctor at Hennebont.'

'What does the plaque on the drawer say?'

'The name of the man who invented it: Peugeot.'

'You're a teacher – show me how to write "Ankou".'

'What a strange notion. I'll try to make the letters for you on this sheet of paper, even though my writing has changed beyond recognition. The ample strokes I used to make when my pen ran as freely as water at the mill have been reduced to painful scribblings. There you are, Madame. ANKOU.'

'Ah, so it's like that.'

Thunderflower sat down on a high-backed bench. With the coffee grinder between her knees she poured a third of a packet in and slid the lid shut. *Clack!* As it closed, the servant's mouth opened, and, turning the handle, she gave her judgement: 'This is a better method than the old one, where I had to use a hammer to smash the beans wrapped in a cloth. Sometimes a few would escape and fall on the floor so you had to hunt for them if you wanted to grind them as well. It wasted time.'

She listened with relish to the merciless cracking sounds of the machine's internal workings, which ensured that not a single bean was spared.

'Monsieur Kerallic, I've spent so much time at the bedsides of so many people, taking care of what needed doing to them.'

'Are you a nurse as well?'

'No, I wouldn't go that far, but even in the time between leaving Pontivy and arriving here, I had three years in farms, inns, and bourgeois households, everywhere wiping the brows of people so racked by convulsions that they ended up as dust.'

'Death in every place? You have to agree, Hélène, that's a real catalogue of disasters.'

'You could say that, couldn't you, Monsieur Kerallic? I go into a house and everybody starts to vomit.'

'Maybe they'd swallowed something harmful. Did no one suspect anything?'

'You can't tell what's in a soup just by looking at it.'

'What do they die of?'

'Chest digestion, I expect.'

'Chest digestion?'

The servant's Bretonisms and her Morbihan peasant accent amused the old teacher, who was looking closely at her in an enigmatic way, his eyes as gentle as two flowers on a heap of rubble.

'You've seen a great deal of misfortune. No one could have such bad luck.'

'I force myself to carry out my work.'

'Yours is a sad profession.'

Thunderflower went on turning the handle of the coffee grinder as she talked.

'At all events, it's not for the money that I go to this trouble. Besides, I've very often left households without getting my wages.'

'Why? Were your employers poor?'

'It's not so much that but ... as I told you ... often when ... left ... they ... weren't al ...'

Words were missing from her mouth the way notes can be missing from a keyboard.

'What can I do, Monsieur Kerallic? My weakness is growing too fond of people. But it's true that I've seen the deaths of so many people caught up in my destiny. And it's not over yet ...'

With her mind in disarray, she poured more roasted beans into the grinder while the old man grasped her meaning.

'It's the same with me: I didn't become a teacher to grow rich. But when you feel a particular calling ... And speaking of yours, I read in yesterday's issue of *Le Conciliateur* that the Emperor Napoleon's ashes are being returned to France. We owe him two million deaths.'

'How many?' asked the cook, stunned and suddenly humbled.

'Two hundred thousand in Russia, forty thousand at Waterloo ...'

Thunderflower was dumbfounded. 'I don't know what he was cooking, but he did a hell of a job of it! I myself find the best thing for cakes is *reusenic'h*. It has a sweetish taste. At one point I thought of anti- ... -coin? ... -note?'

'Antimony?' the teacher suggested.

'That's it. But people would have noticed the taste of tainted silver and said to themselves, "Oh, this cake tastes funny, I'm not going to finish it." How many is one million dead?'

'That's as many dead as there are grains of coffee in the drawer of that grinder – you should open it, by the way, because it must be full by now.'

The servant took a pinch of brown powder between two fingertips, and let it trickle on to the sheet of paper with ANKOU written on it. Using her nail she pushed a good score of the grounds to one side, before comparing it with the heap remaining in the drawer.

'No ... you're having me on, Monsieur Kerallic.'

'It's true, Hélène.'

'How could that be possible?'

'Ah, how it *was* possible ...'

'You're getting muddled, my dear Monsieur. It's time I gave you your mixture.'

She nipped into the kitchen; there was the sound of a singing kettle, then the dull 'pop' of a cork being removed from a bottle, soon followed by the clinking of a spoon stirring something. Thunderflower came back into the room carrying a steaming cup.

'But then with your Léon Napo, there – the human coffee grinder – France became very, very great.'

'He left it smaller than it was when he came to power.'

'Is France far from here?'

'We're in France, Hélène.'

'No, no, it's Brittany here. Oh, my poor Monsieur, you're not very well at all now.'

The old teacher raised the cup to his lips, blew on the steam then took a mouthful. The servant watched, asking, 'Is it to your liking?'

'A bit sweet but I was expecting that. Thank you for making it for me.'

'It's the least I can do. A small service is never refused.'

'Delighted to have met you, Hélène.'

'Likewise.'

'You're very good at your job.'

'Thank you. I don't often get compliments.'

A fog was spreading over the humble schoolteacher's eyes; he had been a young man at the time of the French Revolution, with eyes as blue as a summer's sky.

'Monsieur Kerallic, may I cut a lock of your hair? I always like to take a keepsake with me when I leave, so I can add it to the previous ones. I'm making them into a garland and keeping it in one of the compartments of my bag.'

The elderly gentleman showed his assent by extending two fingers on the hand holding his cup, then taking another long draught of the coffee while the servant cut one of his white curls. Next she placed the sheet of paper with the name Ankou written on it upright against the old man's chest. 'So they'll know who's done this to you. Of course your doctor won't believe it – he'll think the coffee has burned your stomach. Doctors are asses, easily fooled.'

'I'm grateful to you, Hélène, because finally I'd had enough of the circus of civilisations and of this life, a dirty business with never-ending cares …'

His breathing was growing laboured and his voice so weak that his words barely reached her ears. Facing Thunderflower, whose eyes showed a rare gentleness, he was smiling, having placed his empty cup on top of the volume of Celtic tales. He called her 'Maman' by mistake, and recounted a memory from his early childhood. 'I was scared of the big shadows. I was scared of the way the sun moved around in the evening. Farewell, you who brought my death into the world.'

'*Kenavo*, Monsieur Kerallic.'

'Well now, Madame Aupy, are we going to eat this soup or what?'

'It's sweet.'

'That's because it has carrots in it and carrots are a bit sweet. Are you afraid I might poison you? I'm not Léon Napo. Who's that in the drawing on the wall opposite you?'

'That's my son François — he's a priest in Orléans. I'm so proud of him but I don't hear from him any more.'

'He's got an unusual face and a very big nose, hasn't he? Eat up, Madame Aupy, another spoonful — for François!'

Lorient

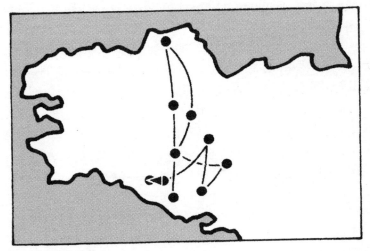

'Euark! Euark!'

'Monsieur Matthieu Verron, do you think your wife's cough sounds like a cock crowing? Because if it is like a cock's crow – all the medical books say this – then it's a croup cough, and then, well ... But *does* it sound like one? I can't quite make up my mind.'

'Euark, euark!'

In the well-lit dining room, expensively furnished in pear and cherry wood, a woman was lying flat on her back on the rosewood table, arms by her sides. She was dressed in an apron with a large silk embroidered bib, and a neck trimmed with swansdown, and lay with her head resting on a pillow, pale and ill, suffering from acute pains in her chest.

'Euark, euark!'

'It's not exactly "cock-a-doodle-do",' said Matthieu hopefully, as he stood next to his wife.

On the other side of the table, the doctor did not know. Monsieur and Madame Verron's cook, motionless at the dying woman's feet, ventured no opinion. She was content to admire the husband, seeming to find him as handsome as a pale god with ivory eyes. He, his long light brown hair in a ponytail, registered absent-mindedly that a button had come loose from his blue Glazik waistcoat, two more had fallen off and were lost, and there was a tear in his shirt cuff.

'These accidents to my wardrobe happened when my wife suddenly clutched me, and cried out, "Matthieu, I love you."'

At the mention of this cry, the cook bit her lower lip and shook her head, while the doctor wondered aloud as he sounded the sick woman's chest. 'What we need to understand before we have any hope of curing her is this: is your wife really coughing or is she trying to vomit? Is the complaint coming from the respiratory system or the digestive system?'

'Just now, after afternoon tea, she suddenly brought up a small cake.'

'It would seem to be a stomach problem then. Was the cake bought in town? Perhaps it was bad.'

'No, carefully prepared by Hélène.'

Hélène. Matthieu Verron had spoken the servant's name. How sweet it sounded to her ears. She wanted to hear him say it again.

'Who are you speaking about, Monsieur?'

'Why, you, Hélène.'

The cook lowered her eyelids with a sigh of pleasure. Meanwhile, Madame Verron was not in a good way at all.

'Euark!'

'Oh, now her nose is bleeding,' said the doctor in concern. 'It must be the lungs then.'

'Maybe not,' her husband cautioned. 'My wife sometimes has nose bleeds because the scent of flowers is too strong for her. We didn't have a single one on our wedding day. She's particularly sensitive to wild flowers, like the ones that grow on the moors round the menhirs. She attributes malign powers to certain flowers, as if they'd made a pact with evil.'

The doctor glanced around to check. 'I don't see any flowers in this room.'

'Quite. We've never had a vase in the house.'

Thunderflower turned her head towards a rain-streaked window, and saw a butterfly waiting patiently on a branch. Her heart was heavy. The branch dipped, and the husband said, 'Strangely, my wife's nose bleeds began again a few days ago, without her smelling the slightest scent of flowers. It coincided with Hélène's arrival in our house.'

'Whose, Monsieur?' asked the servant.

'Yours, of course.'

The cook pulled a face, disappointed that her ruse did not work every time.

'Eu-eu-eu-euark!'

The air was still, and everything seemed to hesitate. Could this cough be compared to the song of a gallinacean or not?

'Eu-eu-eu … Eueuark!'

'Co-co-co … Cock-a-doodle-do!' echoed the doctor. 'It's the cock crow,' he cried, suddenly panicking. 'The poor lady won't recover.'

The husband took hold of his wife's hand and squeezed it.

'Oh, no, don't die, my darling. With your last sigh the sun will go out, and the stars will be thrown from their paths. Never could I forget or replace you.'

Thunderflower, lids lowered and breathing fast, drank in the words, apparently imagining they were addressed to her. Her heart was beating like a drum while the wife's stopped beating altogether. The dead woman's hand slipped from the widower's fingers. Matthieu Verron took the band from his ponytail, letting his wonderful hair hang over his shoulders as a sign of mourning. Outside, in the rain, two crooked fingers knocked at the window on to Rue du Lait. They belonged to the two Norman wigmakers. Enquiringly, the tall one-eyed man made scissors movements with two fingers, while the short misshapen one rubbed his thumb against two fingertips on the same hand to signify that they would pay for the lovely head of hair. The doctor's palm slid over the dead woman's face, to close her eyes.

'It was an attack of croup, the most acute I've ever seen!'

The widower buried his face in his hands, alone in who knew what depth of sadness.

'For her funeral I shall have to stipulate "No flowers or wreaths."'

Thunderflower's dreaming gaze was lost in the distance.

A few nights later Matthieu Verron was unable to sleep, alone in his marital bed. Face to the wall, curled up like a foetus in his inconsolable widowhood, he had left the candle burning on his bedside table. He thought he could hear the staircase creaking as if someone were coming down it towards his room – then the door opened. Matthieu turned his shoulders and eyes to see a long white wisp, like a woman's ghost. An apron with a large silk embroidered bib, a neckline trimmed with swansdown ... Transfixed by what he saw, Monsieur Verron thought he was dreaming. The creature approaching him was like a fairy descended from the mountains, and would soon take on mythical status. She had hips broader than his wife's and her heavy breasts emerged, bright as eyes, when she let her clothing slip to the floor. She had blond pubic hair and her nakedness was infectious. Matthieu took off his nightshirt. The newcomer joined him in bed, immersing herself in his shadow. Between the slipping sheets, their feet felt for one another and their hands trembled, knowing each other near. Beneath the stars, it was a curious journey the apparition took to the widower. Was it not also shameful and distressing? The burning candle was like a silent reproach. He tried to put it out but it always came alight again. Joys and mysteries, alternately dim and brilliant waves on their bodies – the night was a confusion of illusion. The pair of them were like two beautiful pink gods dancing naked. Blooming with sensuality and alive (her!), endlessly alive, there she was gliding the tips of her breasts, her parted lips over Matthieu's chest, down his stomach and further, begging, 'Please ... Give me something to put in my mouth.' Then there came very great happiness, true intoxication. She knew how to imitate the whirling tongues of the angels. He cried out loudly in gratitude.

At breakfast time, the servant brought him a cup of chocolate and asked, 'Did you sleep well, Monsieur?'

'I had a dream, Hélène.'

'Oh, that's nice.'

With a simple lace cap on the back of her head, the blonde girl served the widower at table and stood behind him. While waiting for his bath time, she rubbed his hands and feet with a herb that grows at the bottom of springs. 'That's what we used to do at Plouhinec to banish heartaches.' It neither helped nor harmed him. He could feel Thunderflower's fingers and the satin-soft skin of her palms, and breathed in her vanilla scent, sweet as a secret. All day long she was modesty, calm, respect, silence, attentiveness, quietly doing her humble duty as maid of all work, but come the night ...

The door of Monsieur Verron's bedroom opened. Here was happiness again. Lying on his back, Matthieu turned joyfully towards the naked fairy who was drawing nearer. She straddled him, seating herself on his hips, upright in the saddle. In the handsome widower's night she opened an escape route towards the ideal. She moved up, and down, and up ... His eyes and fingers took their fill to the sound of celestial harmonies. Hearts chimed! Full in the golden glow of the candle, she laughed and bent towards Matthieu's mouth. Between her lips he could see the pearly tips of her white teeth coming nearer, and drank in her breath; oh, the sweetness, oh, the poison. Even as he filled her with tenderness, so many steamy kisses, suddenly, joining their delirious hands, the pale lovers cried out as one. She flung into his throat dizzying words, risen from the depths of the earth, which turned everything upside down: 'I love you, Matthieu!' and in response he called out the name of his dead wife. Raah!

Ashamed of his error, he pulled the sheet and coverlet over them both, throwing the fairy, so expert in the wonders of the universe and matters of love, in shadow. You may imagine what pleasant secrets were harboured by the cloth and wool as they moved together like waves. They shared a perfect orgy whose vices would have outraged savages, before a gentle hammering resumed.

'Did you have a good night, Monsieur?'

'Lovelier than I've ever dreamt of. What about you, Hélène? Did you sleep well?'

'Monsieur is taking an interest in my dreams now? Might he be considering proposing marriage, thinking me a suitable match?'

'Would I be making a mistake, Hélène?'

'Yes, Monsieur.'

That evening, in the attic above Monsieur Verron's room, Thunderflower was pacing up and down, holding her head in her hands and pleading, 'No, not him, not Matthieu!' But *squeak, squeak*, in spite of her fingers in her ears she could hear the squeaking of an axle, which brought her back into line: 'Think of your duty! As for that old irony – love – I'd really like you to think no more about it. It's an illusion.' With her soul in torment, when night fell she listened to the voice speaking to her from the depths of a horrendous pit, plaguing her so much she was like a desperate woman in her attic room. 'Not him …'

On the floor below, Monsieur Verron was in bed, eyeing the ceiling and hearing his cook's buckled shoes trailing over the floor. He tossed and turned, unable to sleep, his heart gripped by anguish, when, with the approach of dawn, his door finally opened. The apparition who brought a touch of the supernatural into the widower's life had changed from day to night. Her eyes were eyes no longer, but two small white candles burning deep within two big black holes. She was like a shipwrecked woman in a nightmare with no shore, but who had been led to him by some alien force.

'It's over. We won't see each other again.'

She was dressed, and carrying a bag over one shoulder. He got up, naked, to face her. 'Sweet death, I would have surrendered myself to your arms ...'

'Don't say anything.'

While she let him slip her camisole off over her shoulders and take down her petticoat, a sigh from the beauty's lips punctured the silence: 'You'll forget me. I will have been only a passing shadow.'

Kneeling opposite him she took a bottle of white powder out of one side of her bag. She appeared to sprinkle it over something. 'Quench me,' she demanded, then put it into her mouth whole.

He could see her back view reflected in a mirror hanging on the opposite wall. The sweet thing's shoulders, her neat waist, her backside, broader because it was resting on her heels, made the shape of a guitar. At the top of this instrument of pleasure, a blonde head was swaying back and forth and he caught hold of the hair to impose a rhythm on it. Handsome conqueror filled with light, pure as an angel; as dawn came a transparent farewell dripped into his mouth. Pale tears with iridescent reflections streamed from feminine orifices.

*

Thunderflower stumbled across the ill defined and badly paved Rue à l'Herbe, both arms wrapped around her stomach. She was pale, choking, vomiting against walls, blaming it all on the arsenic. She was like someone born goodness knows where, who would soon be found lying dead of despair on the ground. The respectable people who passed her felt ill at ease. The servant hoped that one of them would dare to call her names. And not for the first time … But we mustn't think too highly of Thunderflower. Woe betide all those who would open their doors to her deadly career. In spite of her unsteady state, she walked resolutely towards crime, bag on shoulder, even as she bawled her love sickness. Between the wood and daub houses, which sagged and gaped in the lane where the façades would have merged into one another without the inclusion of horizontal beams, the two Norman wigmakers spotted a triangle of blue sky.

'Look, it'sh shtopped raining!'

'As it is, the shower will have lasted for five years. Look how our cart and its load are dripping.'

Tears were streaming from the forty-something cook's eyes.

'It'll pash,' promised the short wigmaker.

'It'll pass, it'll pass …' repeated the tall one, doubtfully.

Ploemeur

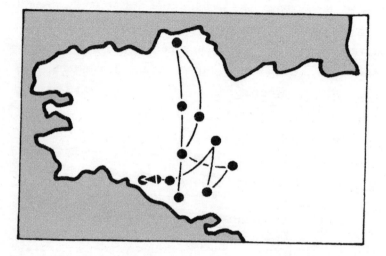

'No, Monsieur de Dupuy de Lôme, I am not happy to stay here until the summer. It's too far to walk to the town of Ploemeur for the provisions. Lorient was where I was taken on. If I had known I was going to end up hanging around a manor house in the depths of a forest I would have turned the job down. I have only one wish, to hand in my apron.'

'You can't do that to us, Hélène. Who would make our meals? The time to refuse was when we informed you we'd be coming here for part of the spring. How do you expect us to find another cook now? It's true, we did say two weeks and now we're staying longer but even if it is a long way for you to go for provisions —

and I'm very sorry about that – it's a pretty place. Just listen to the different varieties of birdsong, the buzzing of the bees …'

'It's poisonous here, the water is polluted and the air is bad.'

'What nonsense is this? I was born in this castle twenty-five years ago and I know perfectly well there are no health hazards here.'

'What's going on, Stanislas-Charles?' asked a man coming into the kitchen, alerted by the sound of raised voices.

He had a white beard along his jaw, curly like a sheep's fleece, spiky hair swept backwards and bushy eyebrows.

His son answered, 'It's Hélène making one of her scenes again. Pah, I think it will be easier for me to build the first steam-powered warships and pioneer dirigible airships than ever to exercise authority over that cook. Not content with complaining about how far it is to go shopping, here she is demanding we go back to Lorient because life here is "poisonous".'

'It is worth noting,' the elderly man conceded, 'that at the beginning of the year our horses did die because of the poor quality of the water.'

'Ah, what was I saying?' exclaimed Thunderflower, standing opposite a sulking Stanislas-Charles, while a two-and-a-half-year-old little girl tugged at the servant's red skirt, asking, 'Are you cross, Godmother?'

'Marie, stop calling her Godmother,' said the young naval engineer in irritation. 'She's not your godmother, she's the cook.'

'She is, Uncle, she's my godmother. Waaaa.' The child began to cry, while her mother ran towards the cook, wanting to know what had made her child – who was wearing a white pearl-embroidered dress with a lace collar – cry.

'Give her to me,' she ordered her brother.

Stanislas-Charles Dupuy de Lôme got hold of his niece, who was hiding in Thunderflower's skirts, and handed her, arms waving, to his sister, while the cook muttered, 'A woman should never let anyone pass her child to her over a table.'

'Why is that, Hélène?' asked the mother.

'It's a sign that the child won't last the week.'

The prediction cast a chill, which the grandfather with the fleecy chin tried to dispel. 'Get along with you, Hélène. You moan but I'm sure that any minute now you'll be off to get one of those plump hens you do so well, either in a fricassee or succulently spit-roasted with potatoes.'

'If it's not too heavy,' the servant cautioned. 'Otherwise I'll get six artichokes between us and serve them with a herb vinaigrette, and that will do very nicely.'

'Personally, I'd have liked trout,' chimed in a bird-like grandmother, joining the others around the table. 'Admittedly to find a fresh water one you have to go much further than Ploemeur, but—'

'As for you, Hortense-Héloïse, don't make things worse,' interrupted her husband, knitting his bushy eyebrows.

'But, Father, why shouldn't Mother be allowed trout?' said Stanislas-Charles angrily. 'It's unbelievable. Are we going to have to take orders from the cook, no longer the masters in our own home? Hélène, you will listen to me and there's an end to it.'

'As you wish,' murmured the servant, only half liking her employer's tone. 'Fine, fine, I'll do whatever I have to.'

'That's it, do whatever you have to. It will make a nice change. You can start by giving my niece her breakfast, and then off you go, shopping, double quick.'

'Be careful, Monsieur Dupuy de Lôme. Go on playing against yourself and you'll end up winning.'

'And no threats either, thank you.'

Everyone left the kitchen, except for Marie, who went back to clutching Thunderflower's skirt. 'Will you tell me a story, Godmother?'

'Of course, dear.'

Wearing a ruched cap, and an air of niceness for the child's benefit, the cook had her back to her, stirring a little milk heating in a saucepan. 'It's the story of a king, the uncle of a princess,' she told her. 'He takes a handful of dust and throws it into the air; his castle falls down, with the princess in it.'

The servant left the manor house, built in the classical style, with her empty basket in her hand and curses on her lips. The early morning insects with diaphanous wings, fluttering butterflies and clear sky brought infinite variety to the delights of the landscape. The sunny day was the finest in a decade.

'In the shentury, no doubt,' gasped the shorter wigmaker, punching the air with his twisted arm, as they stood beside their cart stopped at the roadside.

'Maybe we should unfasten the horses somewhere and let them dry off,' suggested the taller, bald one. They had both aged considerably.

Mist was rising from the fields and the road leading to Ploemeur. The streams were in shade. Further on, Thunderflower passed a farmer busy undervaluing a girl who was being offered to him in marriage, in order to get a more considerable dowry: 'She's really ugly.' The parents handed their eldest daughter a spade and she demonstrated her strength by digging out huge clods of earth. The peasant hesitated.

On her way back to the château de Soye, basket of artichokes on her arm, the servant spotted a small cart being pulled by some men. It was carrying a husband who had let himself be beaten by his wife. She passed a bank with plumes of yellow broom and topped with blackberries, and as soon as she entered the drawing room of the manor house, Thunderflower saw people bending over a little body lying on the floor and rushed forward, shouting in Breton, '*Quit a ha lessé divan va anaou!*' ('Get off the corpse – she's mine!')

While the naval engineer was still asking, 'What's that mumbo jumbo she's saying?' the servant dropped her basket and knelt down beside Marie, lifting her into an embrace and whispering in her ear in Celtic. 'A bad angel made our paths cross. Tell me, at least, I'll have lived in your heart.' The infant put her weak arms round the cook's neck, replying in words no one could make out. It was like the soft sighing of the waving grass, and Stanislas-Charles, uncomprehending, said in astonishment, 'Is Marie speaking Breton?'

Thunderflower's hands closed the eyes of the child in the pearl-embroidered dress. Her mother was prostrate on a chair.

'To what irresistible force has she succumbed?' lamented the grandfather. 'When my son-in-law hears the news he'll be in utter despair over his daughter's death.'

The grandmother could hardly breathe. The uncle looked inside the basket, then at the cook, who was already making for the door. He caught hold of her by the sleeve. 'You should have brought six artichokes, one for each of us, and yet you got only five. Why? You don't like artichokes, is that it?'

'Yes I do, but I don't like weighing myself down unnecessarily.'

Stanislas-Charles looked her straight in the eye. 'Hélène. What did little Marie Bréger die of today, 30 May 1841, at the age of two-and-a-half?'

'You're asking *me* that, when I was away on an errand when my godchild collapsed?'

'She was not your godchild. She was my good niece, when she was alive.'

'That's one person fewer. Blame can go to the saucepans, which have just been recoated with tin, or the poor quality of the water here at château de Soye. Monsieur Dupuy de Lôme, your suspicions will not make me lower my eyes in shame. I won't blush either, do you hear?'

Half demented, the child's mother got to her feet and began to sing. She was filled with the joy of the Church and lit household candles as if they were the tall candles of an altar.

'I warned you we needed to go back to Lorient,' Thunderflower reminded them. 'The weakest has already died, and it will be the others' turns next. I wouldn't be surprised if there were an epidemic soon. The manor house will be left empty, just as has happened elsewhere. The cemetery at Ploemeur will be too small.'

The servant who could predict the future was standing

proudly in front of a chestnut cupboard with ornately carved foliage, while all those around her were agog, hanging on her every word.

'Mark my words. I'm warning you, if we stay here you're all going to die.'

Stanislas-Charles gave in. 'We're going back.'

'Finally ...' breathed Thunderflower. 'The lengths you have to go to in order to be heard!'

Port-Louis

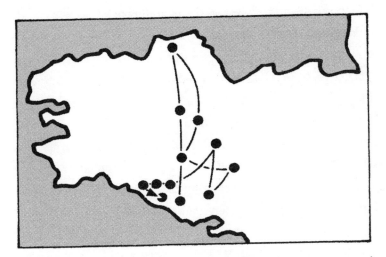

'Sardines, get your sardines! A mackerel too, rays, a tuna, oh, beautiful lumpfish!'

Beneath a rampart decked with pennants, a fishwife climbed back out of the hold of a small boat, barefoot, streaming with seawater, and yelling, 'The catch is in at Port-Louis!'

On the quayside, fishermen in canvas waistcoats and long sailor-style breeches were gathering up the leaping sardines that had escaped from their baskets beside the mooring bollards. Ancient seadogs with weather-beaten faces were chatting and smoking their pipes, never tiring of watching the fishing boats come and go, and the warships in the basin.

Once past the large port ropeworks, Thunderflower turned

down an alleyway and emerged inside the walled town where large numbers of sea birds were flying overhead. In the corners of the fortifications, there were still women selling wild flowers. It was late in the season and they had lost their bloom but retained a rare and lingering scent.

'Next to virgins, the rarest things in this town are stars in the daytime and roses in winter.'

A man was standing in the porch of a house with a criss-crossed gable covered in whitewash mixed with shells, a low door and a single window near to a flaking sign with a mermaid painted on it. He was shouting at a half-naked and decrepit pauper woman. 'I can replace you easily enough! Look at what you've turned into. We could call you *Catel-gollet* (Catherine the ruined), what with your messy hair, breasts hanging halfway down your stomach and a face that would frighten small children. You no longer have a single customer, and what you bring in doesn't cover what you eat. Your cooking's disgusting, and when you do have a couple of sous you drink them!'

Thunderflower looked at the shouting man. He had an unusual face and a very big nose. She had seen him before, she thought.

'Who's the master here, you slut?' he repeated to the pauper. 'What's his name?'

'You, François.'

'François what?'

'François Aupy.'

'So who is sensible and knows how you ought to have behaved under my roof?'

'Maybe—'

'No maybes! Me, François Aupy. I have absolute authority at *La Sirène*,' he concluded, slapping the wall of his wretched establishment with his palm. The weathervane on the roof fell down. Part of the porch collapsed. The man was wearing a cassock patched up with a hundred scraps in different shades and, at his wrists, lace cuffs. He had a straw hat with a yellow velvet band round it.

Thunderflower remembered. 'That's it, it's coming back to me now! You're the son of Madame Aupy at Hennebont.'

'Have we met?' asked the man, turning towards the beauty with the bag over her shoulder.

'I saw you in a drawing at your poor mother's, while she was eating her last carrot soup. You're no longer in Orléans?'

'Well, no. I'm a defrocked priest and here I am, a brothelkeeper. Has my mother died?'

'I was her cook. I'm looking for work. I've been given to believe I could turn up pretty well anywhere in Port-Louis and be taken on.'

'Would you like to work at my place? You do grasp that at *La Sirène* it wouldn't just be a case of scrubbing saucepans?'

'What would you like me to grasp, dear Monsieur?'

'In a military brothel-tavern there's a bit of love on the menu as well. Would you be amenable to that?'

'I'm not opposed to a little bit of courting.'

'I hope you haven't got a sweetheart who'll turn up here one day and make a fuss.'

'Where love's concerned, no one's holding on tight to my dreams any more.'

'François,' said the diseased wretch, who was still there beside them. 'If you replace me and send me away, I'll drown myself in the harbour.'

'That'll be food for the crabs and lobsters then. Piss off, *Catel-gollet*!'

The poor woman with the ravaged body went off, shunned by the merry soldiers she passed. There were so many soldiers in the narrow streets of the fortified town! Uniforms sporting shiny metal buttons, stout black shoes, polished boots. Through a crowd of stalls laden with spices, fabrics from the Compagnie des Indes, tobacco from America, Chinese porcelain, a troop was passing …

'May I introduce your future lovers?' said François Aupy, gesturing towards them. 'They use the old convent as barracks when they're home from fighting or from the colonies. You can imagine that after three months at sea they're particularly ardent.'

'My cakes will calm the troops as well.'

'Strange woman with your green eyes and white teeth, who are you?' Intrigued, the pimp was suddenly familiar.

'What do you want me to tell you?' came the rejoinder. 'My past? That would bore you, and with good reason. My present? What's the point, since I'm in it. And my future? Let's leave that be. My existence is neither happiness nor misfortune. You just have to get used to it, it's a life. Why are you no longer a priest?'

'While I was at Orléans, I was talking about Breton legends to the Bishop. He said, "You who believed what too many people in Brittany are in the habit of believing – namely that there really are female creatures called fairies, who people claim are made of flesh and appear to their lovers at will, taking their pleasure with them and then disappearing when they so choose – do ten days of penance with only water." I got fed up with that so I came here to Port-Louis and opened *La Sirène*. Do you want to sign up then?'

'If your terms are to my liking.'

'By God, you'll have your share of the catch.'

'How do you divide up the takings?'

'In four parts. The boat gets one,' he said, placing his hand on the wall of the brothel. 'I take two since I'm the captain.'

'So I'd get a quarter of the fish.'

'You get the picture. If that suits you, it's agreed.'

'It suits me.'

He held out his two hands to her, saying simply, 'It's a deal.'

Thunderflower crossed the threshold. It was an instinctive movement for her. A fatal force, as involuntary as the giddiness that draws one towards an abyss, made her regard this precipice with curiosity. 'I'm getting old, but here I shall still be beautiful.'

A cook first and foremost, she noticed verdigris in the saucepans, and a pan full of revolting, mouldering stew, and only then the canopied bed opposite the window in this cave of hell. François Aupy went off to find a sergeant in the street.

'Come and see my lodger.'

'That awful *Catel-gollet*? You must be joking ... My men haven't wanted her or her rotten stews for a long time.'

'I've taken on a new girl. She's not exactly sixteen either, but still easy on the eye and she's come at a good moment. Come with me.'

The officer allowed himself to be led by his striped sleeve to *La Sirène*, where Thunderflower was bending down in front of a table to pick up bellows and some logs from the earthen floor. The defrocked priest casually lifted up the Plouhinec woman's dress to above the hips. She had no undergarments on. The garrison sergeant's jaw dropped at what he saw.

At nearly forty-three, Thunderflower still had an adolescent body; petite, her buttocks now parted as if in invitation. Slender thighs tapering to the back of small knees. Further down, the barely defined attractive calves descended to slim ankles. The vertical bar of a chestnut-brown bush was topped by a little black sun.

'Well, Sergeant?' asked Aupy.

'Striking, Monsieur, striking. What a target!'

The military brothel filled with the din of the men as Thunderflower let herself be tossed from one to the other as if by the sea. The way she made herself available might be thought reprehensible but she knew exactly what she was about.

'What are you doing in that part of my person, my handsome warrior?'

'A finger guided me there.'

Of an ancient race, she looked at them, unseeing, with her eyes of stone. Her beauty was on the wane but these men admired her, with their eyes round like those of the Huns! The obliging hostess went along with the games each of those sensual, coarse soldiers liked to play.

In his brothel, François Aupy jingled the coins he had received in his hand, making it clear who was boss. Next to him an army doctor was seated at table, tasting the contents of a dainty little bowl made of Asiatic porcelain.

'That's delicious! What's in it?'

'A carrot purée to make the soldiers wait patiently.'

'But the hint of bitterness I can taste?'

'The cook squeezed the juice of an orange into it, mixed with curry powder she bought at the back of the Comptoir des Indes.'

'It's a ... treat.'

While the doctor proceeded to fill and light a hashish pipe, the pimp boasted about his staff.

'Yes, Hélène's talents aren't confined to the bedroom department. Having her here for the last year is such a stroke of luck for business. And you haven't yet tasted her famous cake with crystallised angelica and raisins that she's made especially for the afternoon's next clients. But she's decided she'll give this dessert only to people who tell her stories while they're in her arms.'

'What sort of stories?'

'Tell me about the wars, Brigadier ... while you have a piece of my cake. Have you ever killed anyone?'

'Killed anyone, blondie?'

The brigadier plunged back into his past as if a chasm had swallowed him up.

'I left a trail of bodies wherever I went. Where I've come from, my business was killing, not this tick-tock clock stuff. Spread your legs. I fought without pity or remorse. I love slaughter, and this cake. Is there rum in it?'

'Yes. Is it all right with you if I lie on my back so I can look at you? Think of more memories.'

'I love the texture of your skin. I finished off wounded men, went after booty, fought with sword and fire.'

The brigadier was inside Thunderflower, still chewing, when he raised one hand. The lines on his palm – the life line, the luck line – were like branches whirling around in the air of the brothel. He opened his hand wide, then suddenly folded in his fingers, roaring as if he had a knife in his hand. With this sudden onset of digestive trouble, his face and eyes were afire, and discoloration already apparent elsewhere. His clenched fist fell back down, sending waves along the sheet on top of the bed.

An adjutant sitting on the edge of the bed frame observed: 'The brigadier's given it all he's got. How he yelled when he came! He'll sleep like a log from now on, you'll see. Come here, my lovely, it's my turn now.'

The lodger of *La Sirène* snaked her pretty young back towards him, asking, 'You've no objection to angelica in pastries? Are you home from the colonies?'

'I led one of the assault troops that took Constantine.'

In a few words he evoked a tropical landscape, then ate a little of Thunderflower's cake before continuing, 'Ten thousand pieces of artillery thundered on the condemned city with no let-up and no mercy until there was nothing left but an enormous heap of dust. Squeeze up so my guts can get close to the bottom of your spine.'

When she requested he be more specific – oh, her charms, her amorous postures – he told her about a chasm that swallowed up a battle front, an earth maw that in one go downed cavalry, infantry, canons, buglers, drummers, the din of the skirmish round the standards, the way a warring multitude was suddenly swallowed up by Death in the intestines of the abyss. The adjutant was developing stomach ache, but insisted, after another mouthful, 'No matter who my country employs me against, I'll joyously and blindly accept this glory, because I love the medals.'

'Hah, people give you medals because you kill, do they? They don't drive you out shouting "Dirty bitch! Lily liver! Evil Breton! Sick bitch, be on your way! *Ki klanv, ke gant da hent!* Ankou, Ankou!" Have you never heard that?'

'No, but I've seen rosettes of fire exploding from walls crushed to dust. I've smelt the gold powder of their pollen, which smells like you,' he added, sniffing her between the thighs. 'Up a bit.'

When she lay on her stomach, Thunderflower's backside was like a young boy's, but as soon as she raised them, her hips became extremely female. The adjutant would have liked to tell her about wars in which troops wallowed in mud, the myriad vicissitudes of his daring career, his lengthy campaigns and extravaganzas of murder in equatorial nights, the sound of fists breaking teeth. He would have liked to tell her of rough horseback rides in Africa while he rode her, but … a strange malady was eating at his entrails, and he collapsed on to Thunderflower's back like a colourful carpet in a souk at Bab el-Oued. The woman of Plouhinec freed herself from the burden, and as her fair hand caressed the spiky hair in forgiveness she was already enquiring, 'Who's next?'

'This galumphing sailor coming towards you, taking off his sailor's breeches,' replied François Aupy. 'Not a pretty sight, certainly, but with a body built like that there'll be staying power.'

'But look how big he is. My fingers wouldn't go round his mast.'

'On board the ships he's known as Attila's Sabre.'

'Ho hum, what a strange lover. He'll do for my purposes, though. Right, you're a sailor, are you? Tell me about the destruction of a wrecked fleet,' she said, slipping one of her delicate frog's legs over the seaman so that she was stuck on to him, as he lay on his back. 'Whew! Have yourself a feast on this triangle of pastry I'm giving you and tell me about vessels lost and men drowned.'

The sailor's neck was thick and pink, with a lace tied round it. Laughing, but giving her nasty looks, he buffeted the whore with his rounded belly like a naked animal. In terse phrases he recounted a shipwreck, the way the vessel tipped over, sometimes covered in spume, cloaked in damp mist, and Thunderflower was drenched in sweat. A rag doll shaken like a soaking floor cloth, she came apart. It did not matter what that oaf inflicted on her (and in what manner!), her body no longer belonged to her. She had left it in Lorient at the home of a kind widower, along with her gift-wrapped heart. As the sweat ran along the blond hair at her brow, she lifted her glazed eyes towards a window pane with fresh water streaming down it, and pleaded, 'Matthieu …'

The other stupid Poseidon suffered from the nostalgia common to military crews. He began describing brass canons at the ready, port and starboard, stuffed full of powder, setting off their broadsides. He himself fired bloody big ones into Thunderflower, who was crumbling. He was indefatigable, ardent as the devil. Wrapped in the sheets or upright against a wall of the bed, he lifted her off the floor without using his hands. She was like a target. And she who could wear out four Hercules, with an undercarriage that was never tired, kept up her role but told him, none the less, 'Have some more cake, a big piece.'

The filthy sailor sank his greedy fangs into it and was struck down, falling on to the backs and bare legs of the sergeant and adjutant, which bounced. That was the end of the party for him. Thunderflower crept on all fours to lean and whisper in his ear, 'Near my home, in the direction of the ria d'Étel, when a fisherman is ill he waits for the ebb tide before he dies.' He looked at her with the burning ecstasy of the first Christian martyred under the wild beast's claw, and stopped moving.

'How strong that little thing is,' said the army doctor at the table approvingly, caught in the sweet intoxication from the cloud of plant fumes enveloping him. 'With her, it's paradise from floor to ceiling. Her bed's never out of use. Here she is with one last one.'

He was so young, curly-headed, delicate and timid.

'This one will give me a rest,' sighed Thunderflower. 'Already in the army, and even in a brothel? You only look about fifteen.'

'When my mother was left a helpless widow, she had to enlist me in the navy early to help her make ends meet, Madame.'

This sort of delicate ship's boy called her Madame and treated her with respect. He did not dare take off his standard-bearer's uniform in front of her.

'It was Attila's Sabre who forced me to come. "Adrien," he commanded, "it's time you learnt to do to women what I do to you down in the hold on the high seas. I'll go first to show you how I stun, joint and fillet females as well."'

'What would give you pleasure Adrien, besides my cake, which is very sweet, just the way children like it?'

'I'd like a taste of that too, Madame,' he replied, pointing to the tart's chest as she wiped herself after the previous client – the hulk who had made her pour with sweat between her breasts.

With her soft, slightly yielding belly, she knelt down, back flexed, leaning towards him where he lay with his head on a sea-blue pillow. Against it the boy's hair looked like the vegetation of an island. His curls made the shape of exotic palm trees growing on a brow of white sand.

'Have you already been to war, Adrien? Tell me while you're eating. It doesn't matter if you speak with your mouth full.'

The standard-bearer's eyes grew wide at the terrifying memories of the disasters he had witnessed at his young age. Through quivering lips, scattered with cake crumbs, he related a series of massacres planned so boldly, executed so coldly and remembered with so little remorse.

Propped up on her arms, one on either side of the youth's shoulders, Thunderflower leaned over him to run the tips of her breasts – as pendulous now as if she had suckled three infants – over the lad's face and eyes, beside his nose, towards his ears and at the corners of his mouth. Her dusky nipples with their broad areolas rolled, folded and bounced as, sprinkling her listening with 'Really?'s and 'Oh, tell me's, she also wandered among the tales of cruelty as if in a beautiful garden. She almost came. An expression of intense pleasure appeared on her face whenever Adrien described the victims' death throes.

'When our captain was killed, he fell into the arms of a sailor, and looked at us, smiling. I was there, I saw it, as I live and breathe, Madame.'

Was it also the gentle tongue of this child-man circling her hardened nipples, his teeth nibbling on them? – Thunderflower came! She pleased him, she felt it lower down as well, and how delighted she was by it! But, you may be sure, her cake was lethal, as that was the end of the young standard-bearer. With white foam running down his chin, he went silent and sad, as very young children do when they are about to die.

'What? I'm not even seventeen, and my life is coming to an end. Mother, you're childless now,' he lamented, with blood boiling. The victim made one last senseless gesture among the lace on the pillow. Thunderflower smoothed out his contorted eyebrows and closed his eyes on his memories.

'You will see no more horrors, will never face the true abyss that the human soul can be.'

A cloud of acrid smoke swirled up to the brothel's low ceiling. Sitting beside the table out of the way, legs crossed and stoned as at Shanghai, the army doctor took another puff on his hashish pipe and pronounced, 'And that little one to end with. Aupy, look how your lodger has exhausted all four. They're asleep around her, in a star shape.'

Head down and red-eyed, the pimp poured himself an umpteenth bowl of cider laced with far too much brandy and raved, 'Hélène is outstanding. I don't know what would become of me without her.'

With difficulty he lifted his addled head towards the still lovely forty-something, seeing her first in duplicate and then in focus. Seated cross-legged and naked as if in the centre of a band of victims of sacrifice, she thought they smelt almost innocent, as she

141

gathered up medals, stripes from epaulettes, army handkerchiefs and tied them into a chain. Upsy-daisy! The pimp stood up, his legs unsteady.

'Come on, soldiers, time to wake up and go back to your barracks. Up we get!'

Going over to the bed, he gave the brigadier a nudge in the back, and looked at the adjutant. 'They're all dead!'

'Dead?'

The news was sobering. The army doctor went round feeling pulses, lifting eyelids, holding a mirror up to open mouths and noting violet-blue patches on skin, then gave his diagnosis: 'Tropical disease. I've known a similar incident on the other side of the world where an entire regiment was wiped out in a matter of hours by a contagious illness. I can't remember whether it was Lassa fever, river blindness, kala-azar or sleeping sickness. At any rate, these four unfortunates must have brought something nasty back with them on board ship. Quick, I'd better rush to put the barracks under quarantine in the old convent buildings, or else the whole of Port-Louis or even Morbihan will catch it.'

He thrust his hands into a basin of cold water and held them against his face to bring him to his senses again. Then he ran out into the lane while Thunderflower got up and began dressing.

'What are you doing, Hélène?'

'I'm leaving, François. I couldn't be happy here any more.'

'You see me in tears over this tragedy that's taken place in my house and you're leaving?'

'My work here is done. I'm afraid popular rumour will blame me over these corpses. Death follows me everywhere I go.'

'But if you desert me, Hélène, I might throw myself in the harbour or fall ill.'

'Have some of this brew I've made. That's bound to make you better, or there's no luck. Is it all right if I tear off and keep one of the lace cuffs from your multi-coloured cassock?'

As night fell, ashamed of her existence, a shrinking shadow carrying a double bag, afraid, hunched over, she slunk along the walls and left the town.

Plouhinec

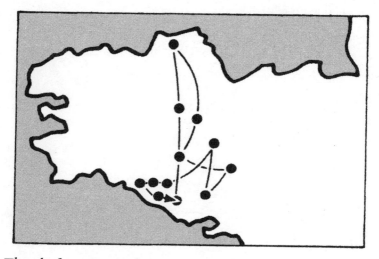

Thunderflower was wilting. Sitting on the Plouhinec side of the wide ria d'Étel, she watched the water go by from her place on the bank of this short coastal river, and gazed across at the village of Belz on the other side. At low tide, the river revealed the expanse of its muddy bed. At high tide, it filled up with seawater coming in from the estuary. Where it met the fresh water from the source of the river, the water became bitter, like Thunderflower, and not fit to drink.

'Well, Hélène, you've taken a long time to come back and see your father.'

'I don't really feel part of the family any more, Papa.'

Jean Jégado, now thin with long white hair, had his face shaded by a broad felt hat and was wearing a tattered canvas smock, which clung to his skin and smelt of mould.

'When I saw you coming, I thought, "Who's that woman? A stranger among all the strangers. An unknown woman, expected by no one."'

Everything father and daughter said, standing beside each other, was in *brezhoneg*. The nobleman who believed he was descended from Arthur or Morgan le Fay was leaning against a tree trunk on which mistletoe grew, brushing the edge of the abandoned church. He was using his sword hilt to knock rusty nails into sprouting branches placed along the broken rungs of a ladder he had found, to strengthen it.

'It's odd, Hélène, that you should come across me beside this old chapel on the very Tuesday I decide to climb up and take some vinegar to the window with our moss-covered coat of arms. I've always promised I'd do it one of these days and then the morning I make up my mind to it, there you are as well. It's funny, isn't it?'

'You might laugh, I suppose. Life is hilarious. All the people whose homes I go into end up clutching their stomachs, it's so funny.'

'Did you hear about the awful things that befell your godmother, your other maternal aunt and even your sister, just like your poor mother?'

'Each time, I was there. They didn't suffer for long. Papa, do you know where I could find Émilie Le Mauguen? You remember, the little shepherdess with the flat face and bulging eyes? I'd like to see her again so I can finish something I didn't know how to do properly when I was eight.'

'The one whose soup you put the whole belladonna berries in? That old spinster left Plouhinec a long time ago to become a day servant in Guern, I think. Whether she's still there I have no idea.'

'Right. That's too bad. Perhaps some other time, if the occasion arises.'

The tide was coming in. Boats tied up and resting in the mud earlier were afloat and moving again. When the tide was high they would be able to go up the river. The sun set the water ablaze. Thunderflower, who was looking pale, shaded her green eyes with a hand in order to see better.

'What a long bridge they've built across the ria d'Étel to Belz, Papa. Did they shut up a live nurseling in one of the piles to ward off ill fortune, since it's said that the first one to cross a new bridge will die within the year?'

'No. Our traditions are dying out. That bridge is new and charges a toll: five centimes for a pedestrian, ten for someone on a horse and twenty for a cart. It's the Pont Lorois, but across there they call it the Pont du bon Dieu for fear that one day the Ankou will cross it from our territory. It was time there was a crossing, though. It's ruined the seamen on their barge, which no one uses any more, but well ...'

Jean Jégado's daughter looked at the stone-clad arches, and the roadway of the structure, which was more than a hundred metres long and four metres wide. Past the toll booth, she saw a rickety cart starting to cross from Plouhinec; it was being pulled with difficulty by two old men.

'I feel better now we've passed that village – my memories of it are not good,' murmured the man with one eye.

The sickly, twisted one lifted his eyes, dark-rimmed in his face with the broken jaw and, seeing something bowling towards them in a cloud of dust from the other end of the bridge, wondered aloud, 'What on earth ish that?'

Pulling the shafts of the rickety worm-eaten cart with its load of bales, they continued on their way. Opposite them, heavy cart horses, in harness, were drawing a carnival wagon at a lively pace. Standing on the vehicle's broad platform, drunk and laughing as he held the reins, was someone disguised as Mardi Gras, clothed entirely in cod tails. He was being pursued by the strident din of a pack of wives and children throwing eggs, sugar and flour at him and yelling, 'Mardi Gras, don't go away, you will have some pancakes! Mardi Gras, don't go away, you will have some chocolate!'

Mingling with these shouts were those of the husbands, who were running and yelling, 'On Shrove Tuesday, whoever doesn't have an ox kills his cockerel! If he hasn't got a cockerel then he kills his wife!'

That Tuesday, 8 March 1847, the procession celebrating the last day before Ash Wednesday left Belz in the direction of Plouhinec, in pursuit of Mardi Gras. The pounding of the horses' hoofs and people's clogs, and the din of the iron-rimmed cartwheels made the roadway of the new bridge shake. The two wigmakers had already ventured some way on to it, confident about the moment when the two vehicles would have to pass each other. 'That wagon is just over two metres wide, and our cart slightly less. There should be room enough to pass.'

There was not. The cart was sent flying through the air like a fairground doughnut. Its shafts slipped out of the Normans' hands and the whole thing went over the parapet, its rusty hoops whirling above the countryside. The short wigmaker, whose nose had been mashed in the accident, felt weak with shock. His hands turned to jelly when he saw the cart plunge into the river, where the current rippled, carrying away the bales of hair. They tore open and gaped, grinning horribly. That was a near lifetime's worth of hair-gathering that was escaping and spreading over the surface of the brackish water, driven by the tide. The ocean wind howled and the tall wigmaker raised his arms, a crazy tree whose twin-branched top encroached on the sky as he yelled at the top of his voice, '*Diskredapl! Diskredapl!*' ('Unbelievable! Unbelievable!')

'What? Can they speak Breton now?' said Thunderflower, beside her father as he picked up his makeshift ladder to lean it against the wall of the former sanctuary.

All that was left on the bridge was a single bale of hair, which had fallen down beside a chain on the huge brass lantern, which lit the cart on night-time trips. While the festal procession was already alighting on the other bank in a cloud of dust, apparently unaware that anything had happened, the toll keepers from both Plouhinec and Belz came running. They were very upset.

'That's the first accident we've had on the bridge.'

'It won't be the last,' promised the Normans, 'if those drunken Bretons carry on driving like madmen.'

The toll keepers offered them their hats as compensation, and the Normans put them on and continued complaining. 'And then there's the communal letting off steam at Breton festivals, God save us. The torch-lit circle of Saint Lyphard, for example, with its effigy of a human sacrifice ...'

'While Shaint Mandez, God alone knows why, ish content with an offering of a new broom. Thish region ish mad.'

Hooking their lantern chain to the remaining bale of hair, and carrying it between them, one behind the other, they continued on foot in the direction of Belz and, in particular, the coast.

'To wash Brittany off your handsh, you really need the shea.'

'It takes that big a wash bowl when there's so much filth.'

The bands decorating their round hats fluttered over their Norman necks as they went.

Thunderflower stood up to join her father by the chapel where the patched-up ladder was propped up under a tall window.

'Papa, before you climb up, have a look at what I've got in the bag you gave me when I was a little girl. There's a bit of tobacco for your pipe – I found it in Port-Louis. That's where I've come from and I'm worn out. It's from the colonies, I can't remember where.'

'Thank you, Hélène,' replied Jean Jégado, after filling the bowl of his old Morlaix clay pipe and taking an initial puff. 'That's tobacco, is it?'

'I think so. An army doctor, who smoked a lot of it, left it on a table.'

'It's a tobacco that makes you drunk. How are you, Hélène?'

'In general I'm at risk of being disgusted with myself. My path is strewn with corpses. I have so little taste for the world of the living.'

'Daughter, in recent years, a priest from Auray – the abbé Olliveau, I think he called himself – police from Morbihan, a handsome widower from Lorient and, just yesterday, soldiers from Port-Louis have come asking me whether I know your whereabouts. Apart from the handsome widower, they've all painted you as a girl for whom hanging's too good.'

'Oh, they're not wrong. People can think what they want about me. A handsome widower from Lorient too, you say?'

'Hélène, when you were a child, did you kill your mother? Things have been so bad with me since she's been gone. Could you be the cause of all my suffering, the most implacable of enemies, worse even than Marianne, the hysterical slayer of kings?'

'Still a monarchist, Papa, though you're living on hand-outs? Here, I've brought you a leftover piece of the cake I baked last week in Port-Louis. You can try it up the ladder in front of the window.'

Carrying a pail of water and vinegar with a real sponge floating in it, Jean Jégado climbed the first few rungs, holding on to the uprights and observed, 'You haven't answered my question, Hélène.'

With his nobleman's sword fastened determinedly to his belt, he scaled the ladder with its several branches going off in different directions, as if he were climbing back up his family tree to the familial coat of arms obscured beneath the sea moss. Balancing his pail against the wall, he held on with the hand holding the piece of cake, and his sponge was already washing the top of the church's principal window. Dribbles of emerald and black were gradually revealing the shape of a vermillion lion on its hind legs, when Jean Jégado heard his daughter confess, 'Papa, I'm weary of living.'

In straw rotted by a stream of dirty water, she related her moral crisis, sitting on one of the bottom rungs of the ladder so that it would not slip. She was watching peasants spreading the moorland with the run-off from a dung heap. Her back to her father, who was right up high, she confessed, 'Papa, since my poor mother used to call me Thunderflower, I've actually become the Ankou. I can tell *you* that because you'll never tell anyone else.'

'How do you know I won't?'

'Try my cake. It's not too dry, is it, even though it was baked a week ago?'

'It *is* a bit, of course, and very sweet, but it's nice. So, Thunderflower, will you be going to look for Émilie in Guern?' Jean Jégado added, the pipe in his mouth giving off acrid swirls.

'No. After what you've told me, the police and all that, I'm going to leave the area and cross the *stêr an Intel* at last.'

At the top of the ladder, Jean began to sweat as he was overtaken by an unquenchable thirst, which he put down to the 'tobacco' his daughter had given him. His eyes were red, and not only from the reflections of the vermillion lion in the main window, now partly washed and with the sun shining on it, and a bitterness boiled his stomach. His legs began to flail about. The hashishin up the ladder – not to be confused with the assassin at the foot of the contraption – swayed towards the glass coat of arms, which suddenly imploded.

'Good, there we are,' sighed Thunderflower, without looking round as her father went through the window.

It was like the splashing of the water when the Normans' cart went into the ria d'Étel. The shards of glass flew out in circles.

Jean Jégado entered the church the opposite way from your normal churchgoer. Head first and pointing towards the floor, he passed a Crucifix whose Christ, he thought, looked a bit crafty.

As for Thunderflower, leaving five centimes at the Lorois bridge toll, she emigrated towards Rennes, muttering, 'My, my, that's another one. And to think it won't be the last …'

Vannes

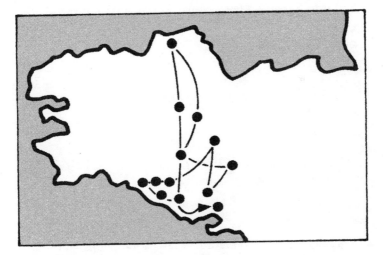

The following day, Ash Wednesday, on a road leading to Vannes, a large woman made of straw covered in rags was being paraded through a village to be burnt in the marketplace. Four thin workmen plus a stocky one with a bare chest, side by side like the five fingers on the hand of a giant, were, together, turning the wheel of fortune on the front of the church, to see what the future had in store.

A priest came out, objecting angrily, 'Consulting the wheel of fortune is now forbidden by the clergy.'

'*Kant brô, kant illiz, kant parriz, kant kiz …*' ('A hundred regions, a hundred churches, a hundred parishes, a hundred customs …'), said the giant's hand by way of justification, spinning the wheel of fortune again, with its twelve little bells, each of which made a different sound.

Next to them, two shopkeepers were discussing the forthcoming municipal elections. 'So, who will you vote for?'

'I don't know.'

'You don't know? That means you're voting for our rival.'

'Maybe.'

'But the man's a liar.'

'Oh?'

'Didn't he tell you he was Breton?'

'Yes.'

'Well, that's not true – he comes from Lorient.'

'And is Lorient not in Brittany?'

'Oh, there's no having a sensible conversation with you.'

One of the pair noticed Thunderflower in a black cape with the hood down over her eyes and her bag on her shoulder. She was at a herbalist's stall, buying a few medicinal plants and looking at the mouldy pancakes on display, which the saleswoman was recommending to her.

'It's a remedy for wounds. Look, I scrape off the whitish film that's grown on the pancake, and slide it into this little jar. You then apply the ointment to a wound. Will you take some of this as well?'

Next the orphan from Plouhinec bought a piece of dried eel, which the fishmonger offered to cut into three. 'It'll be easier to chew.'

The straw woman went up in flames. By the time Thunderflower, looking suspiciously innocent, left the village by the coastal route, the fire was not quite out in the pile of ashes.

*

After passing through the rugged, windswept countryside the gallivanting cook rounded a bend in the rutted track and saw the coastal dunes, and the wigmakers at the edge of a piece of land. Rye, oats or buckwheat would be sown there no doubt, but for the moment it was still bare earth. The Normans were on their knees, breaking up clods with the sides of their hands, and planting the Breton hair from the bale. First they folded each long strand in two. Making a hole in the ground with the tip of a finger, they placed the capillary fibre upright in it. The clay was pressed back around the base, and the long hair, duly planted, would begin to wave, reclining and standing up again with the wind. It was beautiful. The watercolour sky was shot through with the shrill cry of the gulls. A butterfly fluttered by, a stemless flower. In the distance a donkey brayed. So much of Nature was in this vignette. The vivid blue sea and yellow sand shifted. Thunderflower admired the order of things and she understood what the Normans were doing. She knelt down beside them at the edge of the field and began pulling hairs out of the bale and planting them in the ground. Silently, the wigmakers turned their soulful eyes on her. Thunderflower spotted the deep nasal wound that the weakly Norman had incurred at the time of the accident with the cart on the Pont du bon Dieu. She opened a pot and, taking the white foam on her finger, applied it to the scarred wigmaker.

'*Crampöes mouʒee?*' ('Mould from a pancake?'), he checked.

The one-eyed wigmaker offered the unexpected nurse a bottle of brandy. '*Gwin-ardant?*'

She took a long drink straight from the bottle, then gave each of them a slice of her portion of dried eel.

'*Sili mor?*'

In a row from left to right, the Jégado woman, the short wigmaker, and the tall one, chewing the dried eel for a long time, spent the whole afternoon on their knees planting hair without exchanging another word. Before them the ocean was rolling in a bed of golden seaweed. Islets lay on the water like baskets of flowers. A sacred unease was fermenting in the brains of the three hair farmers, longing for the infinite. A smile came over the world, and some graceful sailing boats danced on the horizon. The wind got up. It began to stir the scents of leaves and resin. As evening drew near, at the time the first star rises and work is at a close, countless rocks sprouted among the waves into which the red disc of the sun was sinking. Weary now, the wigmakers put an end to their day's work and stopped lining up their rows of planted hair. Back by the roadside, they lay down on their fronts in the field, without worrying about dirtying their ruined clothes. Thunderflower went over and did the same. Chins on folded arms, they surveyed their handiwork. Against the backdrop of the setting sun, the wind combed, ruffled and smoothed the field's hair. With a tall band of sparkling foam behind it, the meadow found its hair parted first on one side, then on the other. It tidied and untidied its hair to the sound of the waves. Thunderflower and the Normans kept the silence. Faced with the hallucinatory scene, the dreams consuming them must have come from a dark place. Wild geese, cormorants, gulls and herons flew swiftly overhead, making for the fields.

Beside a thatched outhouse used for storing the plough and farming implements, a house door slammed shut as if a storm were approaching. The field's hairpiece was all dishevelled. The two wigmakers were snoring away on the hair bale, near to the chain of their now extinguished lantern. The darkening horizon was echoed in the shape of their folded arms. A sigh deflated Thunderflower's cheek. A death's-head moth flew by.

Fww! Fww!

Thunderflower continued along the coast by night, holding in her outstretched hand the end of the chain of the lantern stolen from the wigmakers, which she was turning around above her head. The big glass lantern, like a coastal beacon, cast large regular circles of light. At each revolution the dazzling flame could be heard hissing – *Fww!* – mixed with the sizzling of the rain that followed, as it changed into streams of white steam. *Fww, fww!* The rusty links of the chain rubbing together creaked like the squeaky axle of a heavenly cart. *Squeak! Squeak!*

Soon Hélène Jégado heard a huge cracking behind her, like a nut splitting open, and then the yells of a ship's crew as they drowned beside a reef. It reminded her of her youth. She did not turn round, but continued on her inexorable way as if hanging on the thread of a star. While the endlessly whirling lamplight washed back and forth over her face, the woman who caused shipwrecks was brushed by the shades of the dead in her mental chaos. Encircled by puffs of smoke rising from her censer in the darkness, pale and tight-lipped, she glanced into the future and saw only despair. Nearby farm-dwellers broke from telling ghost stories to come running out carrying baskets and knives. They passed Thunderflower as they rushed towards a ship that had gone aground.

Late in the afternoon of the next day, still in the rain and seventeen kilometres from Vannes, Thunderflower, who had taken a detour through Auray, pushed open the gate of the cemetery. At twilight, treading between pots of budding geraniums, she was looking for the tomb of Madame Hétel whose last moments she had been forced to miss. Ostensibly seen off by some treacherous soup, the elderly lady with little mirrors on her headdress, the mother-in-law of Dr Doré who had ambitions for the mayorship, had to be there somewhere, but how could she find out where if she could not read?

'Excuse me, Monsieur, could you show me the way to the family vault of Dr Doré, the mayor?'

'Doré? But he was never elected. Something to do with an unfortunate dinner party around ten years ago, I think.'

'Ah? It's actually his elderly mother-in-law's grave I'm looking for.'

'Oh, work it out for yourself,' said the rich man, who was dressed in fine blue linen and carrying an umbrella, as he went off in the direction of some horses with violet accoutrements pulling a funeral carriage. Beside it were some women wearing mourning hoods with trains. Someone else joined them, weeping copiously. Pensive, Thunderflower sat down with her bag on a soaking wet bench off to one side. The rain was sending streams of mud down her cape and dress, which were dirty from when she had lain down in the field beside the two Normans. She was covered in earth like an idol.

'Can I help you?' a man asked. 'I heard you asking the way to an old lady's grave. What's her name?'

'It's not important really. Her mirrors stopped twinkling a long time ago.'

'Have you ever noticed, Madame, that some old ladies' coffins are nearly as small as children's? I know what I'm talking about. My wife and I are monumental masons in Vannes – which is where I'm off to now if you have no need of me.'

'Vannes. That's where I'm going as well, and I hope to get there before dark,' sighed Thunderflower, getting up from the bench.

'On foot, Madame? Would you rather climb up into my cart? The cover would protect you from the bad weather. You'll catch your death in this rain.'

'But I'm all muddy. I'll dirty your seat if—'

'Pah,' said the monumental mason, 'what does that matter? You can dry off and change at our house. If needs be, my wife will make you a gift of some clothes. Here, these are for you,' he added, handing her three roses taken from a wreath.

The itinerant servant was touched by this. 'For so many springs, no one has given me flowers to wear on my bodice. Monsieur, you are extremely kind to welcome me in such terms. Since I'm a cook, I will make *soupe aux herbes* for you, if your wife will allow. That's my speciality, my triumph. There's not a soul alive with a bad word to say about it.'

'Then with pleasure! Off we go. Let us leave this cemetery

where there is no future, and the people here are gathered round that fool who disdained to help you. That kind of mortal's idea of happiness has always made me want to vomit.'

Leaving a half-timbered house in Vannes, under cover of darkness, Thunderflower, dressed in clothes not her own, hurried along a street with a runnel down the middle. Bag over her shoulder, she suddenly heard shouting behind her. People looked up towards a lighted window above a monumental mason's business. There they saw the jerky silhouettes of a man with both hands at his throat, and a woman clutching her stomach, like a shadow play, as the clouds scudded by overhead.

Rennes

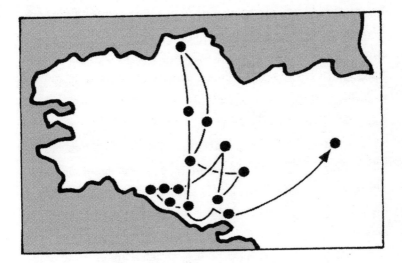

Chantons les amours de Jeanne
Chantons les amours de Jean!

29 December 1849. Death of Albert Rabot. He was nine years old.

Jean aimait Jeanne
Jeanne aimait Jean.

14 April 1850. Death of Joseph Ozanne. He was five years old.

Mais depuis que Jean est l'époux de Jeanne
Jean n'aime plus Jeanne, ni Jeanne Jean.

When on 5 May 1850 Thunderflower arrived at the top of the Lices, in a little square that looked as if it dated from the Middle Ages, she was singing a Breton song from her childhood, and soaked by rain that looked set to go on for ever. The first thing she noticed was the two Normans in the middle, ripping open the mouldering canvas on their last bale of hair. Hurling themselves headlong on their stomachs, they rolled about in the rotting remains of their Celtic hair harvest. They flung grubby balls of lank hair in each other's faces like dirty snow. Their cracked sabots slipped from under them in the mud and again they threw themselves into the long hair from Morbihan, which clung to their bare chests, arms, bagpipers' *bragou-braz* and to their round hats held on by ribbons tied under the chin. With a wondrous hairiness floating over their bodies, which were entirely coated in Breton soil, they were shouting like madmen.

The cook from Plouhinec walked through the square between them, making for the front of a hotel where she asked, 'Is this the *Penn ar Bed*?'

'The what?'

'The End of the World. I want to go right to the end and am hoping the world ends here.'

The servant, descendant of Jean Jégado, seigneur of Kerhollain, who saved Quimper, looked a perfect fright and was doubtless a little drunk. The man she was speaking to put the visitor's dishevelled appearance down to the squally wind and rain, and answered, 'Indeed, this is the hotel known as the End of the World, from the name of this square where in the Middle Ages the town gibbet stood, for executing criminals condemned to death. That was where their careers of destruction ended.'

'Really?'

At the far end of the ground-floor room, whose walls were decorated with stuffed animal heads, a door opened and a voice could be heard asking, 'What has that woman come to say to us, Louis? The one who doesn't look like one of our guests.'

'That she's going to the very end, Mother.'

The voice, which was coming nearer, was the very quavering one of an elderly lady, so stooped she was like a caricature little old woman. Trembling continually, she was supported by a maid who helped her into an armchair.

'There you are, Madame Roussel.'

'Thank you, Perrotte. Hand me my shadowpoint needlework as well, please.'

'Mother, with your illness the needle's going to jab into you all over,' Louis warned.

'Perhaps it will be all right,' said the Parkinson's sufferer, hopefully. 'I would so like to be still again.'

'Give up hoping,' advised Perrotte, the lady's maid.

'Who knows?' objected Thunderflower.

'Thank you,' said the old lady, smiling at the stranger.

Rain was streaming down the windows. In the fading light, the sky gave off waxen gleams that made it look like a shroud. Madame Roussel, who was terribly frail, with her embroidery gesticulating in her hands, looked kindly in her *raie de Baud* headdress with its flounce hanging down over her bent back like a cod tail. Since her back was shaking, it looked as if the fish were wriggling.

'You've fetched up here drenched, but are you hungry?' asked the hotel owner. 'Put down that big bag and at the table you can tell me about yourself as you cut into this round loaf with its golden crust.'

Thunderflower took only a little ball of bread and began working it between her fingers.

'For me, earthly things scarcely exist, and my reality is only in a persistent childhood dream. I heard you were looking for a cook and am offering my services, principally because of the name of the hotel.'

'Yet it's not very enticing,' opined the establishment's trembling owner.

'I see an empty future ahead of me while my past grows ever bigger, Madame Roussel. If you employ me, you, like many others, will taste the specialities for which one day I'll have a truly amazing reputation – *soupe aux herbes* that'll have you falling face first into your plate, cake so amazing you'll be clutching your throat with both hands, and …'

When they heard that, the ghosts of the Druids in Plouhinec, that moor of legends, must have had a good laugh into their green and mauve lichen beards. While Thunderflower spoke about her cooking, she was filled with passion. She moulded the bread into a little menhir and placed it upright on the table.

'Take me on, Madame Roussel. Even if it's for the stupendous wage of five centimes a day, I shan't let you down.'

'That's agreed, then,' said the owner, intrigued, 'but I

personally eat nothing but boiled eggs now, without fingers of bread for dipping. And I open the shells myself — I put the knife blade near them, and it trembles and they break. You take your pleasures where you can find them.' The sick woman pulled a face, while Thunderflower shifted her chair and got abruptly to her feet.

'Oh, no, not boiled eggs. Boiled eggs to be opened by Madame herself! Hélène Jégado serving boiled eggs, and not even spreading something special on the bread!'

She bent to pick up her bag, saying sadly, 'It's a pity because I had hopes about that tremor that bothers you.'

'Tell me about it, Hélène.'

'It's …'

'Spit it out, for heaven's sake. You're killing me with your shillyshallying.'

'I had thought that, with a small dose in my pastry … but if Madame can take nothing but eggs served shell intact, we'll forget it and you can go on pricking your fingers.'

'I give in, you insistent thing, Hélène. Put your bag down again and go and bake me a cake. The kitchen's on your right, you confounded Breton.'

'Will I find raisins, yeast and most importantly rum?'

Once in front of the oven in the Hôtel du Bout du Monde, with the kitchen door shut behind her, Thunderflower took a long swig of rum straight from the bottle. A laugh kept the bottle at her lips. 'Who cares what happens? Let's just drink while the doctors' backs are turned.'

*

'Your mother's not shaking any more.'

'Well, no, Dr Aristide Revault-Crespin. That's because she's paralysed, with her hands stuck round her throat.'

'How did it happen, Monsieur Louis Roussel?'

'I have no idea. Just now, as the night fell, I came back from the hotel stables to find my mother in her armchair, paralysed. Our maid, Perrotte Macé, had already gone to fetch you.'

The doctor, who had arrived with Perrotte, had a white collarless shirt, a waistcoat with wooden buttons, and doubts. He was at a complete loss confronted with the old lady, frozen rigid.

'I'm wondering what could restore her and must admit to a crushing sense of powerlessness. She appears to have fallen victim to a harmful substance mixed with her food. If she were dead, I would ask for an autopsy. Nowadays science is very powerful when it comes to asking questions of a corpse.'

'But she's not going to die. Oh, these doctors!' exclaimed Thunderflower, standing in the open doorway of the hotel, which was very brightly lit thanks to numerous candlesticks.

With her back to the reception she seemed to be watching the square.

'Who's that, who thinks she knows everything better than anyone else?'

'Our new cook. Mother took her on this morning.'

The son refreshed the open lips of his tetraplegic progenitor, with the green tongue and eyes so wide they looked to have been dug out. She remained absolutely still, with her hands at her throat, bent over her canvas, mute and mournful. The lace fishtail of her characteristic *raie de Baud* headdress trailed down her back, but the fish looked well and truly dead.

Beggars were rushing across Place du Bout du Monde, to ask Thunderflower, 'We saw the doctor hurrying here with the maid, shouting "Madame Roussel!" Has the hotel owner died? If she has, you need to give us something to eat. When someone dies, food is given out to the hungry destitute, who come to the dead person's house at night. It's a tradition.'

'Shush, not so much noise, but of course I'll give you something to eat. In any case, I've been waiting for you with this big cake on a plate – it's barely been started. It's better the leftovers go to the poor than go to waste.'

She gave each shivering wretch a ready-cut slice, saying, 'Here, take this but go and eat it further away. I don't want to have to spend time clearing your remains from the pavements.'

She poisoned people indiscriminately and as absent-mindedly as if she were throwing seed for the pigeons. For the men and women returning to the middle of the square, death was on its way. With the light from the hotel behind her, Thunderflower's enormous Herculean shadow filled Place du Bout du Monde.

Dr Revault-Crespin emerged from the half-timbered building, accompanied by Louis Roussel.

'Give your mother a strong dose of magnesium morning and evening,' he instructed him. 'It's an antidote. I don't think it'll be enough but maybe she'll start shaking again.'

He was astonished, then, to see the starving vomiting in the square. One of them was pleading for a drop of water to cool his tongue, as if he were surrounded by flames. At the same time, another finished chewing and in the blink of an eye collapsed as if his bones had dissolved. Their unloved shadows were all writhing on the ground. Like an echo, in the middle of the square bordered by tall houses, their death rattles all merged into one deep sound.

The worried doctor gave his diagnosis. 'No doubt it's the vile cholera returning to Rennes, promising us nothing but a dirty stinking death. There'll be no more murmured complaints from shivering down-and-outs at the corners of the square. They'll fall silent. Good evening, Monsieur Roussel.'

Thunderflower was puffing peacefully at her father's pipe. Beside her, Louis asked, 'Is that tobacco you're smoking? Perrotte claims my mother was paralysed as soon as she'd had some of your cake.'

'If she's said that, it's very wicked,' the cook replied calmly, looking round at the maid, who had stayed in the hotel reception.

Her gaze slid over her. It was the gaze of a wild beast, a big cat, but her voice remained soft.

'You wait, Perrotte, one of these days I shall make you *soupe aux herbes*.'

Splosh!

On 1 September 1850 (the date was written on the front page of the newspaper – *Le Conciliateur* – lying beside her where she sat) Perrotte Macé fell face first into a plate of *soupe aux herbes*. Her forehead hit the rim, and the piece of crockery tipped up. It flew into the air in the kitchen of the Hôtel du Bout du Monde, depositing its green contents on the maid's brown hair then, hitting the neck of the servant stretched on the table with her arms out sideways, it rolled along the curve of her back, bouncing off her vertebrae, and fell on to the floor where it exploded into a thousand pieces. It was like a circus turn. Thunderflower had to stop herself applauding.

Dr Revault-Crespin arrived in the wreckage. His soles crunched as he asked, 'What's happened now, Monsieur Louis Roussel?'

'I haven't the least idea. I was by my mother's armchair, in despair at seeing her still just as inert, when the kitchen door opened and Thunderflower announced, "Perrotte Macé has snuffed it."'

Shaking his head, the doctor walked round the kitchen table. 'Was Perrotte having her dinner?'

'Yes, a simple soup, I think, Doctor.'

'A simple soup. Where's the rest of it?'

'I gave little bowls of it to the town's shameful poor, who came running,' said Thunderflower. 'And, incidentally, they should be grateful to me for doing what I can to help them.'

'And you, Monsieur Roussel? Any symptoms? Do you feel all right?' asked the healer.

'I'm fine, but Hélène didn't give me soup. She cooked me stewed peas, and I must say they were excellent.'

Having been right round the table, Aristide Revault-Crespin slipped a hand into the green slime of the maid's hair, before taking a long sniff at his dirty palm.

'Hélène, does any of these kitchen cupboards contain rat killer that might have accidentally got into the food?'

'Any ...?'

'Rat killer, poison, arsenic!'

'I'm not familiar with *reusenic'h*!' Thunderflower burst out angrily.

'Arsenic,' the doctor corrected her.

'You see, I don't even know how to say it properly! No one can say they've seen any in my possession.'

At the sink the doctor poured water from a jug to wash his hands carefully with soap, saying to Louis Roussel, 'An autopsy would reveal the truth.'

'Perrotte's relatives would never agree to that, sharing the revulsion for opening a corpse that all peasants have.'

Revault-Crespin wiped his fingers on a cloth, and said, 'What if I were to order an autopsy anyway?'

On hearing that, Thunderflower soon vanished. Going down Rue des Innocents towards the banks of the Vilaine, she groaned, 'I was wrong. That wasn't the end of the world.'

'What? What's that, Rose Tessier? You're telling me there's a former judge who's now a law professor at the University of Rennes, an expert in criminal cases, and he's looking for a cook? That's who I want to work for! A specialist in crime. Of course!'

In Thunderflower's enigmatic green eyes, it was difficult to know how much was unbelievable defiance, and how much the desperate desire now really to throw herself into the jaws of the wolf. Sitting on the terrace of a modest bar where the neighbourhood servants liked to get together early on a Sunday morning – their day off – Thunderflower enquired slyly of the woman next to her, 'And where does he live, your …'

'Théophile Bidard de la Noë, tipped to become Mayor of Rennes one day, lives on the riverfront near Pont Saint-Georges.

I've worked for him for fourteen years, first as a daily servant and as housemaid for the last three.'

Glass of brandy in hand even at this early hour, the cook from Plouhinec gazed upon the shimmering waters of the river flowing through Rennes. Reflections bouncing off the Vilaine spattered green, red and mauve light on to the mist-shrouded clothes of the workers who, even on a Sunday, were beginning to unload pottery from Quimper and slates from Redon on to the quayside. Other men crouched down to lift sacks of chestnuts, which they would take by mule to Brest. As they straightened up, their legs cast shadows like bars on to the tall houses on the opposite bank. Thunderflower stood up.

'Right, let's go. Lead the way, Rose. Life is dragging on under this green tree, which, without appearing to do so, is holding on to its leaves!'

The glass of brandy slipped through her fingers to break against the corner of the table and she burst out laughing. Amid the fragments of glass, Rose Tessier drank the rest of her cup of coffee. Round her neck she had a glassware necklace. Ageless and very thin, she looked like a horse the slaughterman has rejected. A bandaged ankle gave her a limp.

'That's from another fall I had at the beginning of October,' she explained. 'I'll fall and kill myself one day.'

Beside her, the servant from Plouhinec was not walking too straight either, which worried Rose.

'Are you sure this'll be all right, Hélène? Monsieur Bidard is very demanding where a cook's concerned. He's already dismissed three since …'

'Oh, when he sees my references …'

'Hmm! Hmm!'

The law professor from the University of Rennes cleared his throat as he reread the single letter of recommendation of the woman who had come to see whether she might suit.

'"Hélène Jégado is an excellent cook. My one regret is that I am unable to keep her until I die ..." That's what I call a glowing recommendation! This missive from the abbé ... Lorho has no date. So, since then?'

'Nothing. I stayed quietly at his presbytery for fourteen years, and have just come from there.'

'Ah, that's what I like to hear. Just like Rose! I'm always wary of cooks who keep changing jobs. They never fail to cause problems.'

'How right you are, Monsieur Bidard de la Noë.'

That's it, Thunderflower! Use the best of your wiles in the pretty art of deceiving a former deputy state prosecutor who takes you at your word.

'Hélène, I have not yet decided whether or not to employ you, but the salary would be forty écus paid at half-yearly intervals.'

Framed by the floral chintz of an armchair from the previous century, the specialist in criminal cases, born in 1804, a year after Thunderflower, looked hard at her standing there before him, her shining eyes glued to his drawing room wall. He could also smell alcohol on her breath.

'Hmm! Hmm!'

He stood up on legs so bowed they looked like the feet of his Louis XV chair, and went to whisper something in Rose Tessier's ear as she was lighting a fire in the grate.

'Do you know this person well? I find her lacking in honesty, and what's more, doesn't she drink?'

The housemaid turned on her bandaged ankle with a grimace of pain.

'That's because on Sunday mornings, Monsieur Théophile, domestic servants let their hair down a little in the bars. It's usual.'

'Hmm, hmm. Today is 19 October. I'll keep her on past All Saints' if she proves suitable.'

'Keep her, Professor. What will people say if you let this cook go as well? Just think, that would be the fourth since Midsummer Day,' remarked Rose.

'Rose! Rose! Rose!'

In the middle of the night, on the dark second-floor landing at Monsieur Bidard de la Noë's house, a sepulchral voice was heard. It was Thunderflower disguising her own as she scratched her nails on her fellow servant's bedroom door. 'Rose … Rose … Rose …' she whispered.

Several times she tried turning the ceramic door knob, but the door was bolted on the inside where a terrified Rose Tessier was sitting huddled in bed, sheets pulled up to her shoulders and a lighted candle beside her.

'Who is it?' she asked, her voice filled with panic.

'It's me, of course, Rose. Don't you know this is what the Ankou does? Before he loads a victim's body on to his cart he always calls them three times. So for you I'm whispering, "Rose! Rose! Rose!"'

'Go away!'

'I can't do that, Rose. It's my mission to carry you off. No more café terraces for you on a Sunday …'

'Hélène, is that you?'

'There *is* no Hélène. There's only the Ankou. That happened a long time ago …'

'But I haven't done you any harm, Hélène!'

'You don't need to have harmed the Ankou for him to wreak havoc. Open the door, Rose, if you dare. Come out of the pond of your sheets, the swamp of your woollen coverlet, the mire of your sweat where you must be making bubbles.'

Naked under a shawl fastened with an iron button, Thunderflower bent to have a look through the keyhole.

'Oh, you've got much fatter since that *soupe aux herbes* at yesterday's lunch, Rose. It suits you. Your legs are a bit swollen, of course, and your throat, too. Oh, you can't breathe properly any more. You'd like to cry out, wouldn't you, but you can't. You want to knock over some furniture to raise the alarm but there's none in your room, and in any case you no longer have the strength.'

'I'm ill …' came a tiny thread of a voice, barely audible, from the poor maid overcome by a nervous complaint, eaten up by raging fire.

'Where's the wound, though, Rose? Late this afternoon, Dr Pinault prescribed leeches and poultices but your condition's worsening. That doctor's a fool. He doesn't know what he's talking about. He says there's no danger. Well, I'd say you're very ill – I even think you won't ever recover.'

A ray of light through the keyhole picked out a green eye floating in the darkness of the landing.

'This night, 7 November 1850, your hour will come.'

The poisoner made this prophecy while she went on scratching at the wooden door with her nails. 'Rose! Rose! Rose!'

With a perversity that was perhaps innate, Thunderflower continued going to ridiculous lengths to disguise her voice while Rose Tessier — teeth chattering with fever and glassware tinkling as her necklace shook — struggled to stand on her still bandaged ankle and attempt an escape through the window. When she grasped the curtains, the metal rail slipped and fell, taking with it a dusty bronze crucifix — useless — which came adrift from the wall and fell with a huge din of metal mixed with the dull thud as Rose Tessier's dead body collapsed, its skull slamming against the floor.

'Hmm! Hmm!'

On the floor below, Théophile came out of his room in his nightshirt to ask, 'What's going on up there? Rose, is that you? Are you all right?'

He climbed on his convex legs through the darkness to go to knock on the door of the housemaid's garret.

'Rose!'

Taking his shoulder to the door, he forced the bolt and found her lying there.

'Rose!'

He covered his face with his hands.

'Rose!'

He went into the cook's room to tell her that 'Rose ...' but Thunderflower was in bed and feigning sleep. Once the former deputy to the prosecutor had softly closed the door again, she scraped her nails on the coarse fabric of her bolster, beside one ear: *Squeak! Squeak!* And she could hear the squeaking axle of a cart disappearing into the distance, weighed down by yet another set of mortal remains.

'My dear and esteemed colleague Baudouin, I have asked you to come to Monsieur Bidard de la Noë's house so as to hear your opinion about his housemaid, whose sudden death leaves me in a state of indecision.'

'Let's have a look, Pinault.'

The elderly doctor, called in to help by his young colleague who was hesitant to issue a burial licence, was wearing a grey cloth bonnet tight over his skull, beneath which longish white curls fell down the back of his neck. Thick moustaches, similarly snowy, bordered his austere face. He entered the drawing room and approached the dead woman, who was lying on a door supported by two trestles, with a sheet covering everything.

'That's the door between the drawing room and the kitchen, which we took off its hinges,' explained the law professor. 'I thought it preferable that Rose's family should see her here just now, rather than in the attic where she … Hmm, hmm.'

Jean-Marie Pinault, a thin and clean-shaven doctor aged twenty-five, explained things to his moustached colleague. 'I came to examine her yesterday afternoon because of the onset of digestive problems she suffered immediately after lunch. I found her racked by stomach pains and vomiting, but I wasn't worried. First I advised a strong garlic infusion, because I suspected the presence of worms in the intestines, then I prescribed the application of leeches and five centigrammes of morphine acetate. I went off satisfied, and then this! I don't understand what happened to her in the night. Have I made a mistake, Dr Baudouin?'

'I don't think so, young Pinault.'

'What happened to her,' an exasperated Thunderflower began explaining from her doorless kitchen, while she looked in her cupboards for the ingredients of a béchamel sauce, 'what happened to her was she fell. You only have to see the lump on her head. That, in the state she was in yesterday ... In any case, she was always saying, "I'm going to fall and kill myself someday." Well, there you are, it's happened!'

'It is true that she had frequent falls and worried about that,' the expert in crime confirmed to the two doctors. 'Just last month she damaged her ankle, and still had it bandaged.'

'That doesn't explain the grotesquely swollen legs, nor the puffed-up throat,' grumbled the old doctor, suspiciously. 'There's still some mystery to this.'

'What have I done with my nutmeg? Ah, certainly there's a mystery,' the cook continued, with her back to them, getting a deep frying pan and heating it on the fire. 'During the night I thought I heard a mournful voice calling Rose, and something scratching at her door. "It's as if the Ankou were coming for her with his *karriguel*," I thought to myself, and then I went back to sleep.'

'So it's the Ankou's fault then?' said the young Pinault with a surprised smile, sceptical as to this diagnosis, which he found rather unlikely.

'My cook is more Breton than French,' apologised the law professor at the University of Rennes. 'Her nights are disturbed by tales from the countryside of Basse-Bretagne.'

'You may mock as much as you like!' scolded Thunderflower as she browned two soup spoons of butter and added almost the same amount of flour. 'I happen to know that last night, at midnight, in the cemetery of the Caqueux, on the moor where I was a child, all the tombs must have opened. Their cursed chapel was certainly lit up, and more than a hundred skeletons came on their knees to hear Death preaching on the altar.'

She stirred the words of her mad tale vigorously, and the flour and butter in the frying pan with a wooden spatula, while milk rose in the bottom of a saucepan.

Thunderflower boiled with anger when she heard her employer order, 'That's enough, Hélène. And shut the kitchen door. Oh, there's not one any more, confound it! Hmm, hmm. We've heard enough of your nonsense about legends concerning death.'

'Nonsense? But, Monsieur Théophile, I live surrounded by shadows, korrigans and fairies. I see them more clearly than I see you. By day, by night, in my sleep, down in ditches, up in the air and the clouds, and I'm certain I'm in the right.'

Continuing her energetic mixing with the spatula to avoid lumps, she came into the drawing room and let rip.

'Nonsense? It's the doctors who talk nonsense. They don't know anything about anything, and believe in nothing. For example, I know that there's a sacred spring near Plouhinec where new mothers come and drink so they produce more milk. When a man drank its waters out of mockery, his breasts got larger. He could have acted as a wet nurse. But just try convincing a doctor of that!' she exploded angrily, looking daggers at young

Pinault, who had disbelieved her story of the Ankou coming for Rose. 'Upsy-daisy, there goes my milk. Oh, there's hardly any left. Too bad, I'll put some water in.'

'Hmm, hmm. I did warn you, she's a Bas-Breton ...' joked Bidard de la Noë between the two doctors, 'so not quite human. At all events, I'm going to have to find a new housemaid because I can't manage without one.'

'I've found you one who seems perfect, on the terrace of the bar by the river,' exclaimed Thunderflower from the kitchen where she was pouring the milk and water in a steady stream on to her mixture in the frying pan.

'Already, Hélène? Gracious, you've not been dragging your feet, have you?'

'Her name is Françoise Huriaux. I'll introduce her to you tomorrow.'

When she had poured in all the milky liquid, the cook replaced the mixture on a low heat and went back to stirring it constantly to achieve the even consistency she desired.

'I have to wait until the sauce coats both sides of the spatula at once,' she chanted to herself. 'Where Rose is concerned,' the woman from Morbihan continued, with her back to the drawing room and eyes fixed on the wall in front of her, 'you might also think of poisoning.'

She herself said that! She was becoming overconfident, but she enjoyed playing with fire.

Elderly Dr Baudoin followed her lead. 'I thought of that as well.'

'I would have let you taste her last soup, so you could check,' went on the servant from Plouhinec, 'but I gave what was left to blind beggars who could donate their useless eyes to the Vilaine fish.'

'Hmm, hmm?' Bidard de la Noë almost choked. 'The villain's dish, you say?'

'The Vilaine fish!'

'Oh, I thought you said …'

Young Dr Pinault was preoccupied, holding a finger to his temple as he gazed at a piece of furniture that the dead woman had polished and that now reflected her corpse, while Thunderflower put on a show of regret.

'That poor Rose Tessier. I used to call her *Rouanen ar foin* (Queen of the Meadows). I did love her, just as I loved that poor unfortunate who died at the Hôtel du Bout du Monde where I was unable to stay. Perrotte suddenly fell into her plate there.'

'Ruptured diaphragm,' Jean-Marie Pinault pronounced automatically, while the cook added salt and pepper to the sauce, muttering to herself. 'Not forgetting a few pinches of nutmeg to give its distinctive taste. Well, this béchamel is more like a roux but it's not life or death. Will your doctors be staying to dinner, Monsieur Théophile?'

The two doctors scratched their heads and thought of other things, while the crime specialist gave a cough: 'Hmm, hmm.'

'You clear your throat a lot, Professor,' observed old Dr Baudoin. 'The start of autumn catarrh, perhaps?'

'No, it's this business that …'

'Madame? Madame! Hmm, hmm!'

'Oh, I'm sorry. Do please excuse me, Monsieur Bidard de la

Noë. As I rang your doorbell, I was watching two old Normans on the river bank. We've not seen their like here for a long time. They're asking passers-by for a lock of hair, then sticking them to their bodies with mud …'

'Madame, have you disturbed me in order to describe picturesque scenes from local life?'

'I am Françoise Huriaux's mother; you engaged her as a maid on 1 December 1850.'

'Ah? Then do come in. How is my pretty little housemaid?'

'Better. In Dr Baudoin's care at the Hôtel-Dieu, finally, after receiving the last rites, Françoise is recovering. Now she's out of the coma, the girl we took for dead is coming back to life.'

'For ever?' This worried Thunderflower, who was sitting on a chair in the drawing room, slipping Rose Tellier's glass necklace through the buttonhole on a cuff from one of Perrotte Macé's blouses.

'Hmm, hmm, Madame Huriaux, tell your daughter we are impatiently waiting for her to return here.'

'Oh, yes,' confirmed the cook. 'Just let her come back …'

Outside, the spring light was slanting through the foliage of a bush, which was coming to life again, and in at the window where it hit Thunderflower's sensitive eyes; she shaded them with her palm. Next she bent down to bundle the necklace joined to the blouse into her bag, which was bursting at the seams, and put it away in a cupboard. Then she pulled the curtains across the panes framing the show of the perpetual rebirth of plant life, which annoyed her.

'I'll bake Françoise a wonderful little cake to welcome her back. It won't fail to make an impact.'

'That's kind of you, Hélène,' said the law professor, approvingly.

'Monsieur Bidard de la Noë,' began the mother of the hospitalised maid, resolutely. 'I'm here to inform you, this 18th day of May 1851, that I wish my daughter to give up her employment in your household. She is handing in her apron. Better that than give up her life.'

The future Mayor of Rennes was flabbergasted. His bowed legs took him to sit in his Louis XV armchair, making it appear to have six feet. He gestured his visitor to a chair.

'Well now, I'm sure you'll appreciate I'm surprised, Madame Huriaux. Your decision is unexpected, but, most importantly, is it Françoise's own? She is of age, after all.'

'Come now, Professor. You know my daughter. You must have realised that at the age of twenty-three she is humility and gentleness but also blissful ignorance. That slight, slender creature is devoid of her share of intelligence.'

'She's an imbecile …' muttered Thunderflower, standing beside the reattached kitchen door, biting into the skin of a lime. 'But she'll be bloody lucky if she never comes back here,' she concluded, swallowing the bitter juice that flowed into her mouth.

She put the citrus fruit down, only slightly injured, on a console table. 'Don't worry, Professor. I've already found you another maid. Her name is Rosalie Sarrazin.'

'Ever more prompt to take action, Hélène!' said her employer, admiringly. 'Four cooks and two housemaids, one dead, inside a year – it's not easy to find suitable domestics. Fortunately it's working out with you. That's something. But Madame Huriaux, you also spoke of "giving up her life". When she's with you, does

Françoise consider me responsible for the sudden breakdown of her health, her dizziness, the difficulty she has in climbing stairs and even holding a needle? Is she of the opinion that I work her too hard? Does she complain about me?'

'No, not about you.'

'Then about whom?'

'Could I speak to you in private, Monsieur Bidard de la Noë?'

Thunderflower took a deep breath. She was beginning to find the mother of the woman who had come back to life a bit too talkative. She would gladly have cooked her a little something to shut her up, but Bidard de la Noë ordered her, 'Go into the kitchen and shut the door, Hélène.'

The servant obeyed. '*Quit, quit, quit,*' she added in Bas-Breton, which might be translated as 'OK, OK, I'm going.' She got hold of a bottle of brandy hidden in one of the kitchen cupboards, and took a swig while, on the other side of the door, she could hear the blasted mother telling tales.

'Lately Françoise would come home on a Sunday increasingly ill. She'd drink litres of water. Her hands and feet were swollen and she'd be tottering about.'

'So the cook's knocking back the brandy but it's the maid who does the tottering.' Thunderflower wiped her mouth with the back of her hand in amusement.

There was a lengthy silence on the part of the former deputy prosecutor, who responded only by saying, 'Go on, Madame Huriaux.'

'Often on her days off Françoise would tell me, "Oh, those herb bouillons of Hélène's, I've had enough of them. Dear Mother, I can't stomach any of what she serves up at meal times. When it's

183

time for lunch or dinner, rather than saying. '*À table,*' she says, '*À l'abattoir*'. Once, when I complained about what she'd made for me, she retorted, 'If you want to be fed like Monsieur, ask him to invite you into the dining room.' When I prefer to go hungry, she goes into my garret and pours oil of vitriol on to my clothes, to burn them." I fear that one day, Professor, you will be telling me my daughter has died in your household.'

Thunderflower was pacing up and down the kitchen, still holding the bottle, and stopped to look at her reflection in the distorting mirror of a hanging saucepan.

'Gracious me, I've filled out a lot. That's no good, I was always so dainty. What I'm turning into ...'

At the age of forty-eight, she lamented, 'We shouldn't have to grow old. The people who cross paths with me are lucky. They escape this shipwreck – except that little trollop, of course.'

Taking another swig out of the bottle, she amused herself by imitating her employer's speech tic.

'So you're drinking, hmm, hmm, Hélène?'

'I worship pure water and its horrors from afar, Monsieur the specialist in crime. Doubtless I'll pay for it some day, but all that is yet to come.'

Fat Thunderflower had to resign herself to the fact that her colleague was not leaving the household feet first. As she heard the law professor asking, 'Madame Huriaux, are you sure of what you are telling me?' she made herself a promise: 'I shall have to get back on form with Rosalie Sarrazin.'

*

'Rosalie! Rosalie! Rosalie!'

A door on the first-floor landing opened soundlessly, and a dressing-gowned Bidard de la Noë slipped into the darkness to listen to nails scratching and something murmuring on the second floor.

'Rosalie I don't know what there is in that garret. Rose died there, Françoise was very ill and you're going to die in there. I wouldn't like to sleep there. Rosalie this is the Ankou speaking to you, tonight Monday 30 June 1851. Rosalie ...'

The specialist in crime slowly took a flannel belt out of the loops on his dressing gown, and rolled the two ends round his hands, as if ready to leap upstairs in the darkness to tie up the cook, and hand her over to the police. But he hesitated: 'Perhaps it's just some morbid Bas-Breton trick. One can't take action on a mere suspicion.'

Tuesday 1 July 1851, 10 a.m. In the still hazy morning sun, young Dr Jean-Marie Pinault went inside to order something at the bar on Quai de la Vilaine, then joined his colleague Dr Baudoin, who was looking at the front page of *Le Conciliateur* on the terrace.

'Thankfully it's not Sunday, because with all the servants gathering here early on the Lord's day, we'd never have got a seat under the tree. What's in the paper? Is the news good?'

'Er ...' Baudoin hesitated under his grey cloth bonnet, tight over his skull. 'I've been reading the speech that Louis-Napoleon has just made at Châtellerault: ... *I have placed myself resolutely at the head of the men of order. I am marching forward without a backward glance. To march in times such as ours, it is necessary to have both a motivation and a goal. My motivation is love for my country; my goal is to bring about the victory of religion over republican utopias, and to act in such a way that the good cause no longer trembles before error* ... Nothing good will come of this kind of language. Something is afoot, something that before the end of the year will cause great uproar and occupy our minds.'

As a waiter brought two cups of coffee to their table, Pinault replied, 'And what do you think about the latest drama at Bidard de la Noë's?'

'In my opinion,' sighed the chief doctor at the Hôtel-Dieu, stroking his moustache, 'the suspicion voiced discreetly after the death of Rose Tessier has become a certainty. And since last night Rosalie Sarrazin also died from ingesting a toxin, there's a poisoner hiding in that house. Events have moved on, and I'm coming back definitively to my initial idea not only in the case of Rose but also in those of Françoise Huriaux and of course Rosalie Sarrazin. The symptoms, their sudden progress, our vain attempts to halt them, the very nature of the sufferings to which the two unfortunate women succumbed, everything points to poisoning.'

'So what do you conclude, colleague?'

'After our cup of coffee, young Pinault, our business on this terrace will be at an end. Our place will be in the office of the state prosecutor, alerting the judicial authorities.'

In a large office with walls and doors dripping with friezes and silly gilded mouldings, above a huge black marble fireplace dating from the reign of the other madman of Saint Helena – how many was it he'd bumped off again? – the hands of the bronze clock showed eleven. Baudoin rushed in, having first taken off his cap.

'Monsieur Malherbe, for a long time I have kept to myself not remorse but regret over the death of a servant in the house of your former deputy, Bidard de la Noë. Today, along with my young colleague Pinault, I have certified the death of another servant in this same house. Both these women were poisoned. My colleague and I are convinced of this. Even if no trace of poison were to be found in the entrails of the victims, we would still believe it was poisoning.'

The state prosecutor remained silent in his armchair facing the two doctors seated side by side on the other side of his desk in chairs with twisted legs. Another, bearded man strolled into the office and, as he passed a bookshelf, turned to say, 'At Bidard de la Noë's? A law professor with ambitions to be Mayor of Rennes wouldn't be messing about committing that sort of crime. Who else lives there?'

'A cook from Morbihan was there at the time of all three ... incidents.'

'There were three?'

'Yes, well, almost ...'

At last the prosecutor Malherbe spoke: 'Monsieur the examining magistrate, rather than going round in circles, you know now where you have to go.'

After Notre-Dame-de-Bonne-Nouvelle had struck twelve for noon, a thirteenth chime rang out. The examining magistrate had just pulled the cord beside the law professor's front door. This time it was Thunderflower who opened it. On the quayside she saw two gendarmes in their blue and white uniforms – bicorn hats, and sword at their waists – flanking the bearded man who introduced himself: 'Hippolyte Vannier, examining magistrate ...'

The stocky man watched as the servant wiped her hands on her apron.

'Are you the cook?' he asked.

'I'm innocent!'

'Innocent of what? No one has accused you. Is Monsieur Bidard de la Noë there?'

'At noon he sat down to a stew of peas. Come back in a little while, and bring a doctor because Monsieur Théophile will no doubt be very ill.'

The madwoman came out on to the granite doorstep and pulled the door to behind her a little way, adding in a low voice, 'He's about to have lunch. He'll fall ill and perhaps die. It's over. He won't last the week. So much the better if he can be saved, but you'll see that he can't and things will go the same way as with the other three. They didn't all die but they were all struck down. Can't you hear a cart axle squeaking?'

The cook continued, 'I'll wait until Monsieur is buried before I look for new employers. This is all just between us, isn't it? No one must hear of our conversation. Do you promise me that?'

Meanwhile the professor of law could be heard asking, 'Hmm, hmm, who are you talking to, Hélène? What's going on?'

'Nothing, Monsieur Théophile. Eat your peas. They're very good,' answered Thunderflower, while the examining magistrate ordered, 'Let us in.'

Bidard de la Noë was seated at table, napkin at his neck, and lifting a big spoon to his half-open mouth when Vannier cried out, 'Don't eat that stew, Théophile! Officers, place that dish under seal.'

The law professor put down his spoon. 'Hippolyte? What are you doing here, and with the cavalry?'

'Monsieur the former deputy, we are here on a difficult mission concerning two domestic servants who have died in your house. Could you see me in your study for a moment?'

They soon emerged again and, accompanied by the police, searched the cook's room, and found inside her bag, in a cupboard, pieces of cloth, and various objects tied to one another into a long string, much to the astonishment of the examining magistrate, who also ordered the remains of vomit found in Rosalie Sarrazin's bed to be placed under a red wax seal, along with a phial of medicine intended for her. Thunderflower was vexed.

'I, too, good Messieurs, have drunk this syrup. I took a spoonful this morning as I had stomach ache, and it didn't poison me!'

Vannier remarked, 'You're in a great hurry to exonerate this phial, whereas since I've been here I've been very careful never to mention poison in front of you. Follow us. I have an order for your arrest.'

With a wild beast's cruelty in her eyes she turned towards Bidard de la Noë, and an everlasting regret rotted on Thunderflower's lips: 'Missed him by a whisker, the expert in crime.'

'Did you sleep well in prison, Hélène Jégado?'

'I'd just given birth, and I was strangling the child, and its lips were going cold in the dream ... I was completely naked, had no body any more, I was too poor.'

189

The eyebrows of the examining magistrate went soaring, and he nodded his head, very slowly, almost imperceptibly, as if his neck were a gentle spring activated by the woman's breath as she spoke. From his seat in a dusty office whose walls were lined with shelves cluttered with files, he looked across his desk at the alleged criminal seated between two moustached policemen, one with his arms folded over his paunch. A door opened and a secretary wearing grey silk cuff protectors scuttled in with a letter — written by the examining magistrate at Pontivy — for Hippolyte Vannier, who began to read:

22 July 1851

Dear Colleague,

At the news, noised at fairs, that a domestic servant with the forename Hélène was being prosecuted in Rennes for crimes of poisoning, popular rumour in Morbihan has taken a lively interest in past events that seemed strange at the time but that never gave rise to any judicial enquiry, and in which a servant also called Hélène, employed in this *département* at that time, was involved. It was noted that in many families who had engaged this girl, one or more persons had succumbed to a violent death (the abbé Le Drogo at Guern, the Mayor of Pontivy's son, so many others … on 31 May 1841, near Lorient, little Marie Bréger aged two and a half, etc.) and the question was raised as to whether she and the servant you have charged are one and the same. No one here remembers the girl's family name but people recall her birthplace: Kerhordevin in Plouhinec. With this information it would be easy to establish whether it is the same person.

Vannier put the letter casually aside.

'Where were you born, Hélène?'

'Kerhordevin in Plouhinec.'

A big summer fly, shimmering green, flew round and round in the air and settled on the nose of one of the policemen, who banished it with an upward blast of garlic-tainted breath. It went to the other officer's hand, which smelled too much of sweat; a movement of his finger saw it off. The buzzing of its flight was irritating. The examining magistrate lifted on to his knees the bag with two open pockets, which belonged to the woman who was looking increasingly guilty. He pulled out the corner of some checked material.

'This handkerchief belonged to Rosalie Sarrazin?'

'Yes.'

The diagonally opposite corner of the handkerchief was tied to a cheap necklace.

'Did this glass jewellery belong to Françoise Huriaux?'

'No, to Rose Tessier.'

'Oh, yes, of course, since Françoise didn't …'

The necklace was threaded through the cuff buttonhole of a white sleeve. He unfolded it. 'Is this one of Perrotte Macé's blouses?'

'Yes …'

The buzzing nuisance of a fruitfly touched down on Hippolyte

Vannier's beard, wandering off among the black hairs. He dislodged it with the back of his hand while investigating what the bodice's other cuff was knotted to.

'Who owned this key? Perhaps it opened a cellar door.'

'Right, that's enough now!' Thunderflower was angry, and stood up to leave. 'And give me back that bag of keepsakes, so that I can go. I've got things to do, you see. I'm on a mission. What are you thinking of?'

Standing, the two policemen roughly forced her to sit down again. The fly buzzed past the cook who, wrists still tied, extended her hands, opening her palms and snapping them shut on the insect like a lizard's jaws. Taken by surprise, the policemen's hands automatically went to their swords and were drawing them as Vannier gestured to them to calm down. The servant pressed her fingers to a place beneath her left breast, grimacing.

'Have you hurt your hand, Hélène?' asked the magistrate in concern.

'No.'

'Why can I see medals pinned to service stripes and army-issue handkerchiefs in here?'

'How should I know? I must have found a pile of them at a harbour somewhere. You're surely not going to spend the whole day asking me questions about goodness knows how many bits and pieces.'

Going through the line of things strung together, Vannier gave a sigh. 'There are sixty of them.'

Beneath his bearded chin he stretched out a little girl's white dress embroidered with pearls and with a lace collar.

'What size would you say this is? I'd say a two-year-old, two and a half, the age Marie Bréger was when she died near Lorient just over ten years ago, on 30 May 1841, in what is doubtless the last crime covered by the period of prescription.'

Thunderflower thought that with the little girl's dress moving in front of his chest, the magistrate looked like a wicked hairy dwarf in disguise, one of those gnomes encountered by moonlight on the moors around the pagan standing stones, the ones who try to make you dance with them until you drop dead.

'Leave me be, you Poulpiquet. You're not going to drag me into your dance.'

Vannier was looking for the start of the string. 'Who was the owner of this ring with a coat of arms on it? Who did this shoelace belong to? You're not risking anything for that because it was so long ago.'

Outside the Palais de Justice in Rennes the atmosphere was like a market. What a hubbub! In this city, which was badly looked after in spite of its inhabitants' booming trade, the crowd that had gathered had their shoes soiled by early December mud. Regardless of the dirt, they all wanted to be at the trial that was about to be held before the assize court of Ille-et-Vilaine. Dress hems were swishing in the mud when a newspaper seller called out: 'The Jégado case in *Le Conciliateur* for Saturday 6 December 1851, fifteen centimes! Only fifteen centimes for *Le Conciliateur!*'

'What do you mean "only"? It's usually five centimes.'

'That will be the price during the nine days of the trial. Since the stunt in the capital – last Tuesday's *coup d'état* by Louis-Napoleon Bonaparte – the entire national press, if it's not already censored or banned, is writing about nothing but the dissolution of the Assemblée nationale, parliamentarians arrested in their beds, the capture of the Palais Bourbon and the barricades going up in Paris against the soldiers. Only *Le Conciliateur* is giving priority to the Breton poisoner and will relate everything that's said at her trial so it will be as if you the reader were there. Fifteen centimes!'

Despite having trebled in price, the local daily paper was selling like hot cakes, as were handbills printed with the words of a song performed by two twisted old men covered in mud with long hair stuck to it.

With his round hat held on with tapes under the chin, the tall one-eyed man was playing the biniou, which he looked to have found in a muddy waste pit. While his left arm squeezed the inflated cowskin bag, his fingers covered any old holes on the chanter, which was, in any case, broken. With cheeks puffed to bursting point and lips too tightly pursed on the mouthpiece, he was quacking out ear-splitting B's. At the opening of the other long tube resting on his shoulder, bubbles of beige liquid clay formed and then burst, running down the piper's back like earthen diarrhoea. It was gross. As for the small twisted one in *bragou-bra*, who was also bare-chested despite the season, he was handing out the handbills with his wrongly set arm behind him. With the other arm he was taking the coins, and whinnying out the story of the heroine of the day through his smashed jaw. It was all badly written, badly played, and sung off-key, but it sold nevertheless. After the fifty-seven quatrains of the interminable lament, they went back to the beginning:

Cheleuet-hui Coh a Youang
En histoer man d'oh e laran
Seanet diar Hélène Jégadeu
E buhé a ʒou lan a Grimeu!

They expressed themselves only in Breton now. Under the vault of the entrance hall in the law courts, pious women (the sanctimonious sort) were selling to those privileged to attend the trial packets of holy dust for throwing at Thunderflower – the person at the centre of the uproar in Rennes and exciting unprecedented curiosity among the Celts.

Inside the second civic chamber with its walls decorated with intricate motifs, and varnished wooden benches on to which the noisy crowd slid, the smells of various fields hung in the air, carried on trouser hems from Ille-et-Vilaine, Côtes-du-Nord, Morbihan and even Finistère. There was also a smell of clay because, over by a wall, a young sculptor with a thin beard and sporting a cap with multi-coloured ribbons was placing his heap of supple, workable clay on the revolving plate of a turntable and adjusting its height so that he could work standing up. A reporter from *Le Conciliateur* stood beside him, notebook in hand, and asked the artist, 'Who is your work intended for?'

The sculptor was about to reply when suddenly the doors opened and the presiding judge entered, flanked by his two assessors, while the state prosecutor general and the defence advocate took up their respective positions. Overawed, the members of the jury – a farmer, a shopkeeper, a cloth salesman, a tanner, etc. – shrank into a gregarious huddle. There was a bunch of blue thistles on the desk of the judge, who gave the order for the accused to be brought in.

That was the point at which a long shudder went through the room, from fat to thin, young to old, bourgeois to daily servants. Here was the woman people were afraid of, who had sent rumblings of alarm along the rutted roads of Brittany.

'Wow!' exclaimed the sculptor, as he lined up his tools on his plate. 'What an air she has about her!'

Thunderflower was frowning, her forehead low and severe; she had become as ugly as a witch escaped from a Breton moor. Her face was partially hidden by the wide hood of a cloak that surrounded her whole body, to the sculptor's delight: 'That means fewer details of clothes for me to shape,' he said gratefully, piling up the heap of clay with his palms, and putting a ball on top for the head. 'Come to that, I could do without this as well since they'll be cutting it off!' he joked, giving the court chronicler a dig with his elbow, which made his pen slip on the paper.

The judge began with the obvious question of identification. 'You the accused, were you not called by your parents Hélène Jéga—'

Suddenly the advocate got to his feet. 'President Boucly, the defence wishes the case to be held over to another session.'

'Does it now? What an idea. And why is that, Maître Magloire Dorange?'

'Huh, yes, the very idea!' echoed the sculptor in astonishment, holding a steel wire – like for cutting butter – with which he was poised to carve into the mass of clay, after shaping the bench where the accused sat, placed on top of a pedestal.

'Oh, no,' moaned the reporter from *Le Conciliateur* on his left, already imagining having to go and tell his editor in chief they would have to put the price of the paper back down to five centimes.

The young advocate, twenty-four years old, with the long hair of a Romantic poet brushing his shoulders, justified his request. 'The first of my three witnesses, Dr Baudin, who was to tell us about the complexities of looking for arsenic in an exhumed body, was killed yesterday ...'

'It wasn't me!' cried Thunderflower.

'... gunned down in Paris on the barricades of Faubourg Saint-Antoine by the soldiers of Louis-Napoleon Bo—'

'What did I tell you? They throw the book at me, whereas Léon Napo—'

'My second witness, the celebrated toxicologist Émile Raspail, was flung into prison this morning ...'

'That'll be my fault too, you'll see ...'

'... in Bourges by the new High Court of the Prince-President.'

'Where's Bourges?' Hélène asked.

'The accused is to be quiet,' ordered the judge. 'And you can drop that hooligan attitude.'

'On 2 December, France was murdered ...' mourned the young republican defence advocate, with tears in his eyes.

'France? But I don't even know where that is. Is it in Brittany?'

The public mocked this piece of Celtic wit by pelting the accused with their open packets of holy dust, which flew everywhere.

'Finally,' coughed the downcast advocate, enveloped in a grey cloud, which he tried to dispel with his hand, 'my third witness, Dr Guépin, who was to give me the aid of his scientific knowledge, has been detained in Nantes in his capacity as counsel general to protest against the violation of the Constitution that occurred in Paris on Tuesday …'

'What a twist of fate! It's true that's a very bad start for the defence, destroys it even,' conceded the court chronicler.

This was not the opinion of the judge, who, after a word or two with his assessors, pronounced on the subject of the postponement.

'Maître Magloire Dorange, the whole of France is currently moved by the *coup d'état*, but the cause of the country is still standing. There are interests common to us all that we must safeguard. Public peace, the peace of our cities, must above all be assured. The tutelary power in society must not abandon its mission. Political providence will decide the rest. As for your experts, only called to give their opinion as chemists, we think that their assistance is not indispensable to you. The trial will proceed. The court rejects your request.'

Extremely disappointed, the novice advocate sat down complaining timidly, 'None the less you might take into account the fact that right now in Paris, where I was born, people like my father, who makes shoes there, are fighting for …' Seeing this, the very experienced prosecutor stood up, displaying the full length of his black robe. He was apparently not at all dismayed by the arrival of the dictatorship and, eyes like a hawk, began harrying mild Magloire Dorange in powerful theatrical tones.

'My dear new colleague, who seem too easily knocked off

balance and rendered silent for one with your role, you are Parisian? And your father is a shoemaker? Well, my friend, rather than wearing out your robe on the defence bench opposite me to no purpose, would you like some good advice? Go back to Paris and follow your father's example on the barricades: make shoes! Ha, ha!'

Some people in the public seats creased up at this. The judge intervened. 'Come now, Prosecutor Guillou du Bodan! A little professional courtesy ...'

Under his breath the journalist was composing the title of his first article: *Little lamb of an advocate to be gobbled up by big bad wolf prosecutor.* The sculptor was spreading out the edges of his clay mound with a boasting chisel to produce a rough outline of his model, seated across the courtroom, while an usher solemnly read out the indictment so people had a better idea of the case being put against her.

'The crime of having administered poison to five people who have died in Rennes, namely Albert Rabot, Joseph Ozanne, Perrotte Macé, Rose Tessier, Rosalie Sarrazin. Also thirty-two fatal poisonings in Morbihan.'

'Not counting those that have gone unnoticed by the law!' thundered Guillou du Bodan. 'Because, gentlemen of the jury, be in no doubt that she has committed many more. We have here the longest female career ever in the history of murder. So we should leave no gravestone unturned and open every coffin lid we come across on her trail of death,' he insisted, in the bullish manner common to all prosecutors, which in him had been boiled down to its most concentrated form.

'Those cases in Morbihan known to us are covered by the

period of prescription …' ventured Magloire Dorange.

'We should mention them none the less, even if it grieves you, my little friend … and submit to most stringent examination the entire past of your client, who is the single most criminal being ever seen on this earth … and a thief as well!'

'Oh, stealing a table napkin, a silk cord and a few handkerchiefs,' countered the defence, putting things in perspective.

As she listened to what was being said about her, Thunderflower, more buttoned up than a priest's cassock, drew her whole hood down over her face. The judge made the two police on either side of her turn it back down on to her back and shoulders. The sculptor thought it a good idea; he could see her features better like this. 'It's funny the way her cloche hat gives her donkey ears to the sides.'

His modelling spatulas – a round spoon here, a sharp point there, loop-ended tools with boxwood handles – twirled between the artist's deft fingertips as he dug more deeply into his material, while President Boucly recounted the misdemeanours of Thunderflower's terrible life, his lengthy sighs mingling with his slow narration.

'Stomach troubles, vomiting, pains in the arms, swelling of the belly and the feet … exhumations that everywhere reveal the presence of arsenic in the corpses … A horrendous series of crimes committed with a cold-bloodedness, a daring, and a perversity that are truly terrifying … Anna Éveno, Louis Toursaint, Julie Toursaint, Jeanne Toursaint, Catherine Hétel, Émile Jouanno …'

'Oh, gracious, another one! And to think that's not the last …'

said Thunderflower wearily, putting her right hand through the opening in her cloak and pressing it under her left breast.

The sculptor appreciated the gesture from an aesthetic point of view, and added more clay to form the clenched hand, which now rested in front of the abdomen. Boucly interrupted his chilling list to whisper to his two counsellors, 'Morvonnais and Delfaut, I note that she frequently touches her chest with a look of pain. What's the matter?'

'Didn't you see it in the case file, President? The examining magistrate also noticed this gesture and had her looked at by a doctor. She's suffering from a sudden malignant tumour in the left breast.'

'Ah? So she'll ...'

Delfaut gave a grim smile. 'That's not what will kill her, President. You know that quite well. Proceed with reading the list.'

'Jacques Kerallic, Denise Aupy ...' Boucly added. 'Even if just in these instances, what have you, the accused, got to say in your defence?'

The tough old bird gave no answer. She remained sombre and silent, with her gaze like an owl's. A big red-faced man sitting in the public gallery was annoyed by this and advised loudly, 'If she persists in playing mute, too bad, stick a ladder in her belly and maybe that will open her mouth at the same time!'

Thunderflower lifted her eyes towards the speaker. Wasn't it a shame to see him alive and well? She looked at him, eyes glinting, as an animal watches its prey. The smile she gave him was an invitation to death. The sculptor noticed the tips of her teeth between her lips. The journalist scribbled about the palpable suspense. The modeller worked the clay. While he was forming the outlines of the bonnet, a phrenologist took the stand to describe the shape of the accused's head.

'Observe the sunken forehead, which gets broader from the base to the top, and the way the temples jut out. Well, I can state that inside such a skull the vertex has a perpendicular cut; the sinciput and the occiput must meet at right angles.'

'Where I'm concerned, the inside of the skull is just Breton clay,' joked the sculptor, starting on the facial features as the phrenologist, whose language could be abstruse on occasion, continued according to the pseudo-science much in vogue at the time.

'Hélène's facial features – the shape of the nose, the eyelids and the lips – are also indicative of an insensitive cerebral organisation, telling us she would destroy anything with equal indifference and no regret – a piece of wood, an animal, a human, anything you care to name. Never will you see the least emotion on a face shaped like this.'

'Right, who is the next witness?' President Boucly asked his assessors. Beneath the sharpness of a questioning eyebrow there was a dull and weary look in his eyes. 'We're rather short of witnesses from Morbihan as most of them were also victims. We had got to the village of Hennebont. Next came Lorient and the highly suspicious death of Madame Verron. Show the widower Matthieu Verron to the stand.'

On hearing the name – the first name, Matthieu, in particular – Thunderflower felt a tingling in her head. Her soul was plunged into despair. When Matthieu took his place before the jury, still as handsome despite the passage of time, in his white collarless shirt and gilt-buttoned waistcoat, she looked at him only surreptitiously, head bowed, and a torrent of tears falling from her eyes. Her nose sniffed. Her lips trembled (which suggested that phrenology wasn't all it was cracked up to be).

'It's only conjunctivitis. It's very common in December!' said the phrenologist, who had gone back to sit among members of the public, surprised at seeing the emotion on the face of the accused.

'Monsieur Verron, do you remember Hélène?' asked the judge.

'I remember her as if she were a name carved into tree bark. My memory of her is ever more deeply embedded within me.'

'Of course! After what she did to you …' Guillou du Bodan inferred.

'Yes, Monsieur le procureur, after what she did to me: with me, she opened a lock like a thief.'

'Ah, what did I say to the defence just now?' crowed Guillou du Bodan. 'What did she steal from you?'

'Something that was beating for her here, inside my shirt.'

'Go on,' requested the advocate gently, standing again.

Thunderflower lifted her right hand to her heart.

'If I could have my time again, I would like to meet Hélène once more. At my house, she had occasional spells of joy interspersed with lengthy periods of despair that had no apparent cause. When I was out of mourning, I once mentioned a plan concerning the two of us, and she burst out laughing. "You must be mad!" she said, with little peals of laughter, then the very next morning she deserted me without a word, leaving me alone with …'

'... an awful stomach ache, swollen limbs, which we can imagine, but from which you miraculously recovered,' the judge sympathised.

'It was she who must have been ill, and believed she was going to die, that poor creature I so longed to cradle in my arms, the way you waken a little girl from a nightmare.'

The crowd on the benches could not believe what they were hearing. 'The wife's poisoner became the husband's lady friend?' People who were unable to admit that agile love is able to grow even on a necklace of wretchedness like Thunderflower's life showed their anger in shouts, oaths and gnashing of teeth. 'The dead are lying under the ground and people are dancing on their graves!' The journalist whistled through his teeth: 'What a *coup de théâtre*, and what a scoop this will be for me!' The sculptor was using a sponge to smooth the wide creases of the dress and shoes below the hem of the cloak, but went back to the face to try to render the distress in the serial killer's absent look. The prosecutor was speechless (which was fairly rare). The young advocate with the Romantic hair considered it unnecessary to say anything more. The journalist was already writing the article that would cause a sensation. The judge decided: 'Right, that's enough for today. The hearing is adjourned. Let's hope that by tomorrow everyone will have recovered their wits ...'

The crowd began to disperse. The men went outside to smoke their pipes. As if she had granite legs in sand stockings the accused remained seated, motionless and glorious for ever, like her miniature replica made of red clay mixed with iron oxide on the sculptor's base. He was spreading out a damp sheet, intending to wrap his work in it to prevent it from drying out and cracking, when the reporter on *Le Conciliateur* asked again, 'But really, what are you going to do with that?'

'I have the next eight days of the trial to make as many plaster copies from this as I can. After the verdict I'm going to sell them outside the courts, among the people selling newspapers and holy dust and the singers' handbills.'

'Are you mad? Do you really believe there are human beings who will want to own a statue of Hélène Jégado?'

Through the glass of a little window behind the enthralled spectators, yells from outside could occasionally be heard in the courtroom.

'*Le Conciliateur* for Saturday 13 December 1851, the second-to-last day of the trial! *Le Conciliateur!*'

'Put her to death, she's a madwoman, she's sick!'

'The only cure for her is the guillotine in Place du Champ-de-Mars!'

'*Cheleuet-hui a Youang!* La, la, la … La, la!'

'She's not human!'

After a week of testimony from experts and witnesses, and of stubborn silence on the part of Thunderflower, the shouts of the crowd still gathered outside the courts filled the pauses, complete with sweeping and dramatic gestures, of the prosecutor general who, at almost six in the evening, was coming to the end of his vehement closing speech.

'In short, as I have just demonstrated to you, gentlemen of the jury, from her earliest years Hélène Jégado has preferred to follow the path of evil. Like each of us she has made her choice. She must therefore bear the full weight of guilt for her deeds.'

He flourished his gown artistically, creating spectacular black billows before stretching an arm towards Thunderflower like a lightning bolt and thundering, 'Expertly grilling and boiling her lethal concoctions in the malevolent furnace of her kitchen, Hélène was wicked from an early age. All her life she has followed the path of crime with a resolute step. Everything thus destines her for the devastating rigours of justice! Finally, before I sit down, I want to address you personally, Hélène. It might still be possible to do something for you if you were prepared now to express repentance.'

'Repentance? I don't know that word,' Thunderflower apologised.

One of the two gendarmes flanking her translated into Bas-Breton, '*Morc'hed.*'

'Ah,' she said with a nod, and remained silent.

'Have you nothing to say, Hélène? You won't give us an

expression of regret? Then I have nothing more to add.'

What a performance from Guillou du Bodan. The public was won over. The defence had its work cut out. When his turn came to take the floor, the young advocate caught everyone by surprise.

'Gentlemen of the jury, I have no desire to refute one by one the charges you have just heard from the prosecutor. Not only do I accept them all, but I think he has omitted many and I would have applauded if he had charged my evil client with yet more shameful deeds and crimes. For she is a monster!'

What a way to start a closing speech for the defence! There was stupefaction amongst the listeners. One man asked his neighbour for confirmation: 'Who's speaking now, the defence?'

'Yes.'

'Shit, you'd be justified in wondering if he's in the right job. The cook won't be getting off.'

Guillou du Bodan was still reeling from Magloire Dorange's opening words, as the defence advocate continued amidst the stunned silence he had caused to descend on the court.

'Listen, gentlemen of the jury! Listen! Do you hear what they're shouting outside the courts? Listen carefully.'

The jurors strained their ears and heard, through the little closed window, distant shouts like 'Old peasant slut!', 'Fat bitch from the sticks', 'She's not human.'

'Do you hear?' continued the advocate. 'She's not human! There speaks the voice of public opinion, as well as the defence here before you this late afternoon. Yes, my client is not human and cannot then be condemned as a human being would be.'

'Not bad,' was the prosecutor's professional opinion, as

he spotted the cunning angle of attack of his inspired young colleague with the Romantic hair, who continued, pointing to the accused in his turn.

'We have here a monster, a phenomenon no less exceptional than the Cyclops or legendary creatures, half man, half tiger. Look at her! Just look at my monstrous client!'

Magloire Dorange had turned into someone exhibiting a bear or a five-legged sheep at the fair. It was as if, at any moment, he would drum up the crowds with his patter: 'Roll up to see the woman with three heads who can jump five metres – but since her cage is only a metre long she'll do five jumps in succession.' He astonished the court by undermining Thunderflower much more than the prosecutor had done.

'Hélène's acts of poisoning are without reason or motive. She poisons people, that's all. She would poison you with arsenic, Monsieur le président and Monsieur le procureur, and she would bake me a little cake as well, even though I'm here to defend her. She kills whoever she comes across. It's a curse. She is no longer a human being. To we who are, she is unfathomable, beyond all understanding. She's a mystery like certain natural phenomena. Gentlemen of the jury, could you pass judgement on the wind, the rain, the snow, the tides, the fairies and korrigans of ancestral legends told on the moors of Basse-Bretagne? Would you give your opinion on the galaxies? And night, day, eclipses, what do you think of them? Are they to be condemned or pardoned?'

The young advocate, with sweeping gestures and wide eyes as if he were in a trance, was improvising for all he was worth.

'My client's name is on everyone's lips, and no one can remember anyone to compare with her. The name of Brinvilliers has been mentioned, but only to add that Hélène Jégado stands head and shoulders above that famous female poisoner. So I have had no difficulty in understanding why, after lengthy consideration of the case in hand, the most learned specialists at the bar have reached the same conclusion. "There's a problem here, some mystery ..."'

As if under hypnosis, he went on, 'Who, which writer might one day be able to tell us the relationship responsible for her crimes? Who will be able to lay bare the consequent logic that has determined Hélène's entire life? For my part, I remain confounded and shall not attempt to stutter some explanation that would satisfy no one. But how can we avoid imagining that when she was very young she suffered a deep mental disturbance, some disruption of the brain, which brought with it a phenomenal lack of sense of responsibility? And that from then on she made her way through life, all alone, as if she had a scythe, to become a figure of terror? For her, our moral compass does not exist. My client, a member of the human race? Be careful, for that is a calumny against humanity.'

From outside, where the night was taking the air, the crowd could see through the little window as the advocate waved his arms like a man drowning in the sea.

'I believe there are creatures for whom there exists, above human justice, a different truth. Beings made like this go directly towards their goal without concerning themselves with obstacles. When Hélène, who has committed countless crimes, cannot kill people, she attacks clothes, or books, as she did at the convent in Auray. And when she can no longer harm people or things, she turns on herself. Because know, gentlemen of the jury, that since her arrest Hélène has developed a terrifying illness in her chest, one that spares no one. She will die of it, because she has to kill.'

Thunderflower – reviled by everyone – listened in a state of languid indifference. She drifted into sleep, one hand pressed to her heart, while the young advocate, dripping with sweat, was getting worked up on her behalf.

'Ah, what am I doing at this moment? Rather than asking you to spare her life, should I not be begging you to take it? For Hélène, your pitiless verdict would mean deliverance from the terrible physical sufferings to come. But no, gentlemen of the jury, you will not do this because you are not murderers! Patiently, obstinately and ceaselessly, Hélène has destined to death all those with whom she has come into contact. Her extraordinary perversity is a madness, but if it is legitimate to protect oneself from a madwoman, is it right to punish her?'

Shaking their heads from side to side, certain jurors did indeed seem to be asking themselves whether … and then Magloire Dorange hammered home his point.

'Make a distinction between the fate you have in store for Hélène and that which you would inflict on a criminal possessed of all his faculties. And then will you hesitate between a dungeon door closing for ever on a curse, and the executioner who kills in public to teach people that they must not kill?'

The argument hit its mark. The advocate concluded, 'The prosecutor asks Hélène to repent. All well and good, but we must allow her time for that. Repentance will not be born quickly in her soul. You know that. Therefore it is in the name of justice that I entreat you to grant her the benefit of extenuating circumstances. Mercy for her soul!'

It was half-past seven in the evening. It was late and everybody was hungry. That day when all the talk had been of poisonings, the spectators' stomachs were rumbling, eager to go and dine, but the representative of the people – worried by the unexpected efficacy of the defence speech – obtained the judge's permission to reply to the defence. So Guillou du Bodan stood up, still just as haughty and didactic.

'I cannot allow to pass without protest the peculiar theories and unsafe assertions that have escaped from a young advocate carried away by his own words. So, the defence conceded the certainty of all the crimes, while the prosecution did not go beyond the stage of probability in some of them. And yet Hélène Jégado is not guilty? But why? The same defence advocate brought as support phrenology, physiology, psychopathology, and goodness knows what else. Gentlemen of the jury, it is easy to lose one's way in the realm of ideas. Nothing is more difficult than to keep to the right path. Fortunately, I have a thread to follow, a sure guide; that guide is the penal code, which punishes murderers with death!'

He displayed his copy of Dalloz to the court as if he were Moses brandishing the Tablets of the Law.

'After that, what argument is left to the defence, the unprecedented number of misdeeds? What a refuge for innocence that is. So because Hélène Jégado has committed more poisonings than any female killer under common law known on earth throughout all ages, that's why she should be pardoned! As if by committing more and more crimes one earned the right to go unpunished. Perhaps I am failing to discern the "poetry" – I don't know what sort, incidentally – that the defence appears to sense in such a litany of murders. My view is that, between virtue and crime, Hélène has freely chosen crime. Let her then feel the full consequences of her deplorable choice, and that's that.'

Despite being mentally exhausted after his inspired plea for the defence, Magloire Dorange claimed his right of reply. 'One sentence, just one sentence, Monsieur le premier président!' Then without even waiting for permission he declared, 'In his disdain for the defence, and blinded by the penal code behind which he is hiding, the prosecutor is refusing to see that for Hélène it's as if some merciless thing had given her a mission, ordering her, "You must keep going, ever further ..."'

It was the end of the session. The verdict was due the next day, Sunday 14 December 1851, starting at noon. People left the court yelling, 'Time for dinner!'

'Unless it's Jégado doing the cooking, of course!'

'Gentlemen of the jury, in my capacity as presiding judge, here is my recommendation for you as you begin your deliberations: above all, discuss things in a calm and collected state of mind.'

He rapped the desk in front of him with the tip of his finger so as to explain clearly to them. 'If it has not been proven to you that Hélène Jégado has committed the acts for which she is blamed, acquit her!'

He thumped on the wood again, a little further to his right. 'If you consider that, without being absolutely devoid of free will, this woman has been blessed with less of it than most human beings, grant her the benefit of extenuating circumstances ...'

He gave another knock a little further along, still going from left to right. 'If, however, you judge her guilty, seeing in her neither intellectual impairment nor ignorance of morality, then fulfil your duty to be firm, and in that case, remember that in order that justice be done it is not enough that sentence is passed; it must also be proportionate to the crime!'

The jury retired. Outside, the December sun was dazzling. At 4.30 p.m. everyone made their way back to the benches. The foreman of the jury, Pierre Boudinot, a Rennes wine merchant, announced the verdict: 'Sentenced to death.' President Boucly asked Thunderflower whether she had anything to say. She replied, 'Those who have condemned me, thus preventing me from carrying out my mission, they will ... repent in the hereafter, where they will meet me again and they will see ... And he'll see, Monsieur Bidard de la Noël!'

Shouts of anger rang out around the courtroom. The condemned woman was led out amid much commotion. Several gendarmes had to stand around her to protect her from the crowd, who would have ripped her to shreds. 'Leave her to us! Give us that bitch, the filthy slut!'

Under her little headdress trimmed with Breton lace, Thunderflower grew quietly drunk on the shrill sound of the two muddy Normans' broken biniou. She made a nice target for the Rennes marksmen who threw rotting sardines and stale brine at her, so that soon she gave off an appalling stench. Insults flashed through the air like lightning, or danced like will-o'-the-wisps. 'Go to the devil, he'll have a job for you!' 'No one will miss you, you nasty piece of work!' 'Poison pourer, the little stars spinning in the sky are closer to us than you are, much closer ...'

As, at the mercy of them all, she was being taken across to the prison on the other side of the square, the shouts grew hoarse around her. The world said she was odious, but what of it? She remained calm amid this hostility, the universal hatred of which she was the object! Her lifelong dream of becoming the spittoon for the maledictions of the universe, fulfilled! Oh, the infinitely pleasing – to Thunderflower – contempt of respectable people making up the feverish and mad multitude of a crowd every bit as ignoble! As soon as they saw her, pilgrims bent the knee and said a prayer. Convulsing holier-than-thou types barked as they tried to empty their slop pails filled with blessed shit over her. It was clear that an abyss had opened up. Like a cloud of squawking crows, lots of men in double-layered waistcoats and round hats swooped towards her, laughing, and giving her nasty looks. Some of them stuck their tongue out, while others made fun of her body, calling her 'ugly' – she who, in the past, with her perfect siren beauty would have had them all falling at her feet. One of them made a show of disgust. 'Put it away, love.'

'Murderer! Worthless piece of muck! Devil's spawn!'

The whole world had deserted her but she noticed Matthieu Verron standing still among the crowd, gazing at her out of the gesticulating rabble. She read the soundless words on his lips. 'We will no longer go walking together on Sundays …'

The words he mouthed had such a perfect meaning and his hands, hanging by his sides, were bathed in tears. His loving eyes were too faithful. Thunderflower, at that moment (how silly), recalled one of Matthieu's kisses on her soft flower of flesh, which would no more open up to love. She knew he would not want to be present at her execution but would go back to his little white house with the green shutters in Lorient and end his days there alone, hoeing his lettuces and his flowerbeds. It made you want to die.

Everyone wanted to see Thunderflower's face better, in real life. Women tried to tear off her Morbihan headdress. The sculptor from the first day of the trial waved his arm in the air, inviting them to admire the plaster copies of his model instead. Beside him the reporter from *Le Conciliateur* enquired eagerly: 'Have you sold many?'

'I wish! Just one.'

First came the external walls with broken bottles along the top, then the thick doors with triple bars on them and then a rusty key turned in a gigantic lock to open the door into a very small space with an old maid hermetically sealed, as it were, inside it. Sitting on the edge of her straw mattress, she looked round, blinking her eyelids in the direction of the smoking candle carried by a warder whose flat face resembled a round cheese alive with maggots.

'Oh, chief warder Michel …'

The waves of light and shade alternately stretched and squashed the shadow of the gaoler's snub nose (he reminded Thunderflower of someone) and that of his thin-lipped mouth, which gaped like a bottomless pit. 'I am here at nine thirty at night to inform you that the Prince-President Napoleon has said he is unable to use his right of pardon in your case.'

'What does that mean?'

'My God, Hélène, it means that you must prepare for death. The sentence will be carried out at dawn tomorrow, 26 February 1852.'

The light from the resin candle made the head warder's

bulging eyeballs sparkle like magnifying glasses, as he added, 'The chaplain, Tiercelin, is in the corridor waiting to come and listen to you.'

'Listen to me say what?'

'Oh, something like, "On the point of appearing before God, etc." It's just a formality.'

Thunderflower kept her eyes on her gaoler's peculiar face. 'Warder, suddenly, as I'm looking at your face, you remind me of someone who used to be a little shepherdess in Plouhinec, called Émilie Le Mauguen. That little girl my own age gave me the poison I used at the start of my criminal career. It was she – and it was very wicked of her – who taught me how to kill people without risk to myself. I think she later became a day servant in one of the villages in Guern. You have to look for her and subject her to the same fate that awaits me tomorrow. Do you promise?'

For goodness' sake, Thunderflower ...

If the poisoner was in no hurry to confess her sins to the clergyman waiting in the corridor, she was very eager to incriminate an innocent woman. That was like her, at any rate. Even after her death she wanted to go on killing, and smiled with a childlike sweetness while the chaplain, accompanied by two nuns, decided of his own accord to come in, as the turnkey made a promise and an offer. 'Émilie Le Mauguen at Guern, you say? Very well, I shall inform the prosecutor general. Now, Hélène, you have the right to a last meal. What would you like for supper?'

Thunderflower did not reply. The gaoler was concerned: 'Are you afraid I might poison you?'

The two sisters of charity on either side of the chaplain each had a lighted candle. Added to Michel's this meant there were lots of lights dancing on the walls of the narrow cell. They reminded Thunderflower of evenings in the farm at Kerhordevin in Plouhinec, where a fire of gorse and cowpats would blaze in the fireplace while her parents told excessively grim Breton legends.

'Whenever they spoke about the Ankou in front of me, I remember how terrified my parents were. When we heard a sound outside repeated three times, my father's long hair used to stand on end and my mother panicked. I could see how important the Ankou was for the family, and I said to myself, "I'll become important. I'll become something that interests them." So I killed my parents, maternal aunts, and my sister.'

Stock-still, Thunderflower looked down at her knees, and her feet resting on the brick floor. She was no longer thinking, but dreaming. 'I became the Ankou in order to overcome my terrors. And then I no longer had any because I myself was terror. "I won't be at the mercy of their fear any more. I'm the one who'll decide." At night I used to go and fill myself with the strength I needed by leaning against a menhir on the Caqueux moor. I could feel its amazing radiant energy deep inside me. My backbone still burns with it.'

'Dubious idolatry ... and a standing stone that ought to have been broken up or Christianised,' lamented the chaplain, making the sign of the cross in the air. 'Now, as for your expiation, you need to—'

'I'm neither exonerating nor blaming, I'm explaining!' Thunderflower interrupted him as the flames' reflections continued moving round the walls and brick floor of the cell. 'My parents' fears made me so afraid. They gave me their fear and the ground was no longer steady. I was too scared during those evenings. It was my fears that did for me. When parents are paralysed by a fear, they do not protect. Children are so impressionable, damn it!' she said, getting worked up. 'In fact, when parents are that afraid they transmit their fears to their young ones and there's no protection any more, is there? And after that …'

In her homespun prison dress, she went on, 'I think it makes perfect sense. When you've been lost in your parents' anguish, you want to be master of it, and you're even prepared to turn into death to do that, and you become invincible. It's brilliant, being the giver of death. Can you understand the path I took to conquer my fear? It's a vertical path. I went upwards. I am death. I'm at the top of the tree. I am the Ankou. I'm in charge and it's amazing. It's another perspective. There's no feeling involved. You're on top. From the top of the tree, I'm the one who's going to frighten people. I won't be afraid any more. I *am* fear. It's fantastic. No more terror; it's you who decides. You're no longer bound by anything. I didn't want any more emotional ties so I said to myself: I'm going to make some *soupes aux herbes* and little cakes. I've been too afraid.'

'But why didn't you say all this in front of the court, Hélène?' said the warder Michel, moved by her words.

Thunderflower scored through the question with a sigh, but when the prison chaplain asked her again if she was ready to ask forgiveness of God, she finally answered the head warder's question: 'Actually I would quite like a boiled egg.'

When her cell was in darkness once more, because her visitors had gone – among them the chaplain, who hid the way he had been sent packing with a curt, 'Goodness, you're starting to bore me' – the poor, sad woman lost in the madness of another era, astray among Breton legends and who had merged with her childhood terror, plunged deep into the ravines of sleep beside a broken eggshell. The night birds sang songs of comfort. The deep wind, come from Morbihan, wept between the bars, it was tempting to think … and soon Thunderflower wanted to have a pee in her bed. She forbade it. 'No, no, I can't,' but the Ankou said, 'Go on.'

'No, I have to get up and use the pail.'

'Stay there. It's fine. Go on.'

'No.'

'Go on.'

On the night before her execution Thunderflower wet the bed. It was the first sign she was human (and about time too).

She had rediscovered that fear from her early childhood as well; it was forbidden by her mother and she had been ashamed when it happened in the box-bed. For the rest of the night she turned over, and over again, always pressing different bits of her rough dress on to the big wet patch to mop it up. For her the final challenge was not escaping death but drying the pee.

Dawn, and in Place du Champ-de-Mars, bordered with chestnut trees and buildings, people in their Sunday best swarmed like walking dead. At the centre of the esplanade, in front of the guillotine raised on a platform so that even those at the back of the crowd could benefit from the coming spectacle, Tiercelin the chaplain commanded silence by lifting his hand then, holding a piece of paper, declared: 'Yesterday evening, Hélène requested my presence in her cell in order that she might express her regret for the evil she has done and her fervent desire to die in the odour of sanctity. In front of Sister Thérèse and Sister Clémentine she begged me to make public her statement of contrition, which she has been unable to sign as she cannot write, but which I am going to read to you. *I, Hélène Jégado, being on the point of appearing before the Almighty, and wishing, as far as it is in me, to expiate my faults, ask forgiveness and mercy of heaven. I willingly offer up my life as a sacrifice to the Eternal Father. I hope that God will grant me the grace to die in penitence.*'

The sun rising above the rooftops extended the shadow of Tiercelin's nose over the whole length of his vestments. In private, behind the inner yard of the prison, there was no need to hold Thunderflower down on her bed to tie her up. The Messieurs of Rennes, of Vannes and of Saint-Brieuc – the executioners – woke and bound her without encountering any resistance. The chief executioner, that of Rennes, said appreciatively, 'If only they could all be so amenable.'

One of his assistants, the executioner of Vannes, pulled the condemned woman's arm behind her back too roughly, and the pain from the cancer in her left breast made her yelp like a wild animal.

'No need to make such a fuss,' said the executioner, who was unaware of her illness.

'Especially after poisoning thirty-seven people,' confirmed the one from Saint-Brieuc.

'Thirty-seven ...' Thunderflower raised her eyes. 'Oh my, the law doesn't know about all my misdeeds. I've brought sorrow

220

and desolation to a much larger number of families than that.'

Her last toilet completed, and having declined the offer of a glass of brandy, Thunderflower, with her hair cut up to her neck and still racked with pain from her malignant tumour, was helped up into the cart (*karriguel*?) which moved off, with a squeaking axle, of course. *Squeak, squeak!*

The gendarmes cleared the area around the guillotine when the group drew near. The crowd, desperate to see, was kept at a distance. On the platform Thunderflower caused astonishment by asking Monsieur de Rennes for a mirror.

'Ha, what a time to beautify yourself!' sneered the executioner of Vannes.

'Women,' sighed the one from Saint-Brieuc. 'Touching up her make-up just before her head falls into a basin.'

'I'd like a mirror, maybe propped upright on a chair in front of the guillotine,' explained Thunderflower. 'When the blade cuts through my neck, I'd like to see myself – me this time – die.'

'That won't be possible,' apologised the executioner of Rennes.

Flat on her stomach with her throat on a semi-circular cross-piece on to which a crescent-shaped frame came down to hold her neck, the victim bore no grudge for this refusal by the chief Monsieur (a colleague?) for whom she felt a burst of human respect such as she rarely experienced. But tough luck, he was her executioner … lifting the lever that activated a spring releasing the blade of the heavy sharp cutter. Man's justice descended upon her condemned head. Thunderflower had been cut down.

*

Since the construction of the medical school at Rennes, which was to open its doors that year, was not yet completed by the end of February 1852, dissections were in the interim being carried out in the ossuary of the old cemetery of Saint-Etienne church. On its grim ruined façade was a bas-relief depicting a figure brandishing a skull and a femur, and a quotation: *Death, judgement and icy hell, man must tremble at the thought of them. He is a fool if through inattention his mind does not see that one has to die.* Not the finest lines of poetry ever written. The statues ornamenting the ossuary were obscene and bizarre.

Thunderflower was obscene and bizarre as well – lying naked on her back on a metal table, missing her head, legs apart and her chest open with her ribs and flesh hanging at the sides. She was like the whore offered in a nightmarish brothel with men in white smocks walking round her.

'Tell me what mad misfortune made your eye burst with a smile of sorrow,' said a phrenologist in an aside, speaking familiarly to Thunderflower's head, which still bore traces of plaster from the mould taken of her face for a medical collection devoted to great criminals.

As he began to saw through her skull in order to examine the brain, another observant doctor standing between the poisoner's thighs, noted: 'She never gave birth, but was not a virgin … Faustin Malagutti, where did that wreath of everlasting flowers come from? It's beside the body, getting in the way.'

'A man from Lorient had it sent for her,' answered the famous professor of the science faculty, attaching copper wires to the corpse's exposed heart, on which he was conducting electro-magnetic experiments.

While he regulated the device linked to the conducting wires, Malagutti heard the phrenologist lamenting beside him, 'That's unbelievable, her skull is normal, which puts paid to the theory of the born killer. She has no bump for crime, just as no one has ever found anyone with the bump for mathematics or business. Idiots and assassins have the same brain as everyone else, which suggests that phrenology is wrong-headed from start to finish.'

The smells escaping from the makeshift laboratory poisoned the air. Through the coloured panes of a small window that was not quite airtight, the fumes spread a sort of terror into the nostrils of passers-by. Just then a sudden shout of triumph shot out of the ossuary.

'Look!' cried Faustin Malagutti. 'Two hours after the execution the apparatus is still registering contractions of the right atrium. Her heart is still beating.'

The doctor came out from between the legs, and remarked of the trace, which the oscillator was producing on the graph paper: 'If you can call it beating. It's more like the last quivers of fear.'

Plouhinec

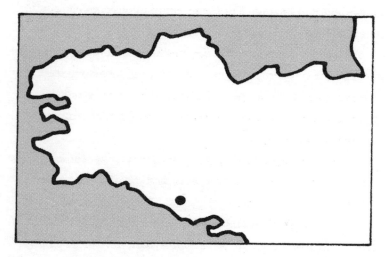

The crumpled front page of *L'Auxiliaire Breton* floated on the breeze as the sun set over the moor. Against the proud outline of a menhir it repeatedly rose and fell, circling the stone and brushing caressingly against it, before moving off. At the foot of the megalith was a heap of blond gorse twigs, like a head of hair. The sole of a worm-eaten sabot came down on a corner of the printed page, which had landed again, with its headline in bold type: A reply by the Mayor of Guern to Hélène Jégado's posthumous revelations.

26 March 1852

Sir,

I was surprised and saddened to read in your newspaper the revelations made by Hélène Jégado in her final moments. She made a most serious accusation against someone in my village.

I have had to gather every possible piece of information in order to discover whether or not these accusations were founded.

I have questioned Émilie from whom Hélène Jégado claimed to have learned her fateful career as a poisoner. I am convinced, both by her replies and by information about this woman from elsewhere, that she would not be capable of that of which she is accused.

She has been employed as a day servant in almost every house in the town, and no one has ever complained about her. There has never been any violent or suspicious death in any of the families for whom she has worked.

Moreover the judge of the appeal court, delegated by the prosecutor general to look into these nefarious revelations, must have informed you that he finds them without substance.

He may also have told you that this pure woman, Émilie Le Mauguen, who is today a poor paralytic with an exemplary life, is still known in Guern as a saint and a godsend to the area.

It is deplorable that before she died, this unfortunate Hélène should have wished to blame an innocent woman for her own crimes.

Le Cam

A very old hand, muddy, wrinkled and covered in extremely long hair, picked up the newspaper page and scrunched it into a ball before wedging it in underneath the mound of straw and twigs forming a pyre around the base of the menhir. The same long thin fingers struck a flint, making a spark and then a flame, which licked the paper, which began to burn, setting light to the straw and the dry gorse.

The sudden blaze lit up an ungodly chapel in the distance with an open door, and a short, crooked, hairy old man with a back-to-front arm, pushing a bewildered woman in a wheelchair. Her flat, startled face – snub nose, eyes starting out of her head – seemed perpetually prey to a fear of invisible forces and of the dark.

At the approach of the female, even though she was paralysed, the menhir glowed erect and pink in the firelight. The damp night air made it glisten and its swelling tip was tinged violet by the dying glow on the horizon.

Grabbed under the arms like a child, the fifty-year-old cripple felt herself being forced out of her chair by four bare arms furrier than a monkey's. She stood upright and panting, supported by two octogenarians – still in great shape, apart from being misshapen – who were sniffing at the flesh of her rump as if it were soup.

Around the megalith, the moor became shrouded in mist, furrowing its brow at the meddling of these Norman ancestors.

The wigmakers, now with long beards, pulled the woman right up to the standing stone. These converts to 'Celticity', thus more Breton than the Bretons, wearing *bragou-braz* and in the case of the tall, stooping one-eyed man, with a broken biniou under his arm, each seized one wrist of the former shepherdess, holding it in a vice-like grip, and they danced! First they jigged on the spot and then in a circle to please the stiff menhir, which was in raptures.

The pale old maid was only vaguely aware of what was happening as she was dragged into the dance round the monument, tossed into the air one minute, feet trailing across the ground the next.

From its place on the chapel altar, next to the statue of the Ankou with his scythe, the little plaster model of Thunderflower – the only one sold in Rennes – seemed to be enjoying the spectacle outside.

To the shrill sound of the tuneless biniou, the men span on the clay ground like Poulpiquet figurines emerging from a *far* cake. Like the bad bearded dwarfs of Celtic legend, they compelled the paralysed woman to keep going. The flames were reflected like candles in the bulging eyes of the servant from Guern and the long hairs caked to the Normans' bodies with mud crackled into red stars with an acrid stench.

While the verbena-crowned Ankou and Thunderflower gazed serenely on, the dancing woman's elbows were kept bent like a drinker's. It was unbearable torment for her. Spinning out of control, she wondered how long she would suffer before it killed her. Over in the chapel, on the thick edge of the granite altar table, these words could be read: 'I will spare no one.'

Round and round went Émilie (for it was she), circling the aroused menhir with the crows in one last delirious dance from which she would never recover. This was her destiny. Plunged into pagan madness, she called on humanity. Anyone passing in the distance would have said he had seen korrigans dancing on the moor. Her pubic bone and coccyx struck the stone and her jaws (which had years ago dodged those belladonna berries in her soup) cracked against the phallic menhir. The erotic structure broke her and carried her away in a mad dance. Under billions of stars, the woman from Morbihan no longer knew where she was.

Held by her sleeves, which wrapped the troupe like a shroud, she opened her mind and legs to the mysteries around her. Sweat poured down on her like cider, the fire was a pancake of light, and as the dance sped up she thought her steaming intestines would burst out of her stomach. Again and again she pounded against the stone until she finally let out a cry in *breʒhoneg*: '*Ya, c'hoaʒh, ya kae! Red-sp . . .*' ('Yes, again, yes, go on! Ejac . . .').

The rain was falling. The fire was smoking. Steam and prickling smuts rose up the menhir, on either side of which the wigmakers in burning *bragou-braʒ* were rolling around like swollen testicles. The cripple fell on the pyre and whoosh! Jets of flame shot up to the violet tip of the megalith and exploded everywhere. What fireworks there were in the darkness. Oh, milky way.

Thus it came to pass that Émilie was laid by a Breton legend, but looking on from the chapel – and with a grateful wink to the Normans – it was Thunderflower's statue that came.

The Suicide Shop

Jean Teulé

translated by Sue Dyson

Has your life been a failure?
Let's make your death a success

With the twenty-first century just a distant memory and the
world in environmental chaos, many people have lost the will to
live. And business is brisk at The Suicide Shop.

Run by the Tuvache family for generations, the shop offers
an amazing variety of ways to end it all, with something to fit
every budget.

ISBN: p-9781906040093 / e-9781906040901

Eat Him if you Like

Jean Teulé

translated by Emily Phillips

A true story.

Tuesday 16 August 1870, Alain de Monéys makes his way to the village fair. He plans to buy a heifer for a needy neighbour and find a roofer to repair the roof of the barn of a poor acquaintance.

He arrives at two o'clock. Two hours later, the crowd has gone crazy; they have lynched, tortured, burned and eaten him. How could such a horror be possible?

ISBN: p-9781906040390/e-9781908313171

The Hurlyburly's Husband
Jean Teulé
translated by Alison Anderson

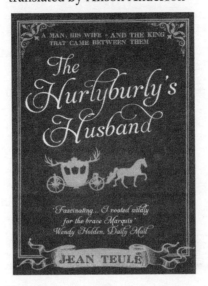

The Marquis de Montespan and his new wife, Athénaïs, are a true love-match – a rarity amongst the nobility of seventeenth-century France. But love is not enough to maintain their hedonistic lifestyle.

When Madame de Montespan is offered the chance to become lady-in-waiting to the Queen at Versailles, she seizes this opportunity to turn their fortunes round. Too late, Montespan discovers that his ravishing wife has caught the eye of King Louis XIV.

ISBN: p-9781906040390/ e-9781908313171/
audio-9781908313799

An interview with Jean Teulé

Jean Teulé tells Christian House how he was warned off researching his black comedy about a 19th-century act of cannibalism

In the Parisian bustle of a popular Jewish pocket of the Marais, a nondescript pair of blue double doors hides a cobbled courtyard at the end of which is a little shop.

In the last century it was a garage kiosk but now it acts as the office of Jean Teulé, a novelist who understands the power of revisiting historical sites for contemporary ends. Teulé invites me into a minimalist space. White walls, bookcase, pin board, iMac, and a neat stack of rolling tobacco. Above his desk hangs a single black-and-white photograph of a classroom of young boys.

Teulé has all the bonhomie and cartoonish delight of a writer in his own little world. He is an idiosyncratic figure on the Gallic literary scene. A London publisher recently told me that he thought French publishing was in a slump. Teulé's bestselling novels such as *The Hurlyburly's Husband*, the story of a lovesick Marquis cuckolded by Louis XIV, conflict with this diagnosis. A cosy looking middle-aged man with an infectious childlike laugh, his appearance is discordant with his morbid, comic dramas. His latest, *Eat Him if You Like*, is published in the UK in translation this week.

Acclamation led him to the source material for his new book. 'After *The Hurlyburly's Husband* had such success in France, I thought people would be disappointed. I thought "I'm going to be lynched,"' says Teulé. 'So I was looking on the internet at words such as "lynch" and "massacre", and fell on the village of Hautefaye.' *Eat Him if You Like*, which tells the true story of Hautefaye, is set over one day of collective madness in the sauna-hot summer of 1870. France was at war with Prussia and the rural inhabitants of the small Dordogne commune were getting twitchy. When Alain de Monéys, a respected local landowner, rode in to the teeming Hautefaye fair he was unprepared for his fate. A slip of the tongue about France's chances and the drunken crowd turned on him. His neighbours became anarchists in their Sunday best.

Passed from pillar to post, ragman to notary, one unimaginable horror to the next, de Monéys endured an extraordinary demise. He was tortured to the bounds of human endurance and then, as he still clung to life, a bonfire was hastily built and he was burnt alive. Insanity, of course, but what has given the de Monéys' affair a particularly ghoulish place in the annals of French history is what happened next. The crowd took his burning fat, an awful kind of human dripping, spread it on hunks of bread and ate him like a party canapé. One reveller crunched on his steaming testicles.

Research was problematic, says Teulé. 'In the village they really weren't happy. They didn't want the story to be known. And to scorn them, I would say, "Well if the book works, I'll open a little restaurant and call it the Hautefaye Grill," laughs Teulé. 'They said on local television that I had better not come back or there might be a second sitting. The current mayor wanted to put up a plaque to say that the village was sorry, but the villagers refused because it was their ancestors who were responsible. The book went out in May, and by August tourists were coming with their book asking: "Is this the village of the cannibals?"' He cackles at the thought, and again when he explains that a Parisian brasserie has already named a dish the 'de Monéys steak tartare'.

Teulé relates to the victim. 'I don't like crowds of people. I'd never go to a rock concert,' he says. 'A few months ago my train was late. After a while, they said that the train could be boarded. Everybody has their place reserved. The train was not going to leave, and yet everyone roared to get their seat. If one little old lady or man fell? I surprised myself by starting to run too. It's that mechanism of a crowd, like the cells in a body.' He believes the Hautefaye story could reproduce itself, and gives the London riots as a case in point. 'Mass can be heroic but it can also be strange and dangerous,' he says. 'That was the same thing. And it started from nothing. Just a little trigger and it blazes into a fire.'

Teulé's milieu is centred on the 'merriment of vice and cruelty'. His novels are bawdy, full of rollicking sex and roiling violence. However, he undercuts this with a graphic humour born of his earlier career as an illustrator. 'When I don't know how to write a scene I will sketch it and put it on my board. I will look at it and the words will come. I can't write a scene if I can't visualise it.' The result is exceptionally cinematic prose. (Teulé's 2007 novel

The Suicide Shop was recently filmed by Patrice Leconte.)

The *petit salon* swirling with cigarette smoke in which we sit is Teulé's retreat from the contemporary world with which he claims not to connect. Yet his private life is one that, at least on the surface, is *Paris Match* material. He is the partner of the celebrated film star Miou-Miou and his oldest friend is Jean Paul Gaultier. He points to the photograph of the Sixties schoolboys and there they are, the juvenile Jean and Jean Paul, looking back at us with beaming smiles. It is the only picture either has in his study.

Teulé might orbit the cultural elite but he's most at home here in his dark corner. 'I love to be out of the world. In my bubble. When I am between two books I don't feel comfortable,' he says. His next bubble is inhabited by the Breton cook Hélène Jégado, who poisoned more than 30 people at random between 1833 and 1851.

'She said that everywhere she went, death followed her. I was in Brittany at a book signing and a baker from Rennes came and gave me a cake saying, this is the Hélène Jégado cake. But without arsenic,' smiles Teulé. He explains that Jégado was executed on his birthday, 26 February. *Extraordinaire*. And once again laughter bursts from Marais's merry messenger of death.

First published in *The Independent*, October 2011